"Maybe you're playing a game, but I'm not."

Lex closed the distance between them, pointing a finger at Grady.

"Yeah, you are, and we need to be honest with one another."

"Here's some honesty." She reached out and yanked the towel off from around his shoulders, trying to startle the calm expression off his face. Why should he feel calm when she didn't? He didn't look massively startled by her unexpected action, but his eyes did narrow a little, so she plunged on. "We are not going out. We are not kissing one another. We are going to retreat to our neutral corners and stay there."

She wadded up the towel and jammed it back at him.

"Whatever. If you need me, I'll be in my corner."

"Why would I need you?"

"One thing I've discovered in life, Lex, is that you never know who you might need."

"And that's where you're wrong. I will never need you." She meant it from the core of her being. Because needing Grady would put her in a very vulnerable position.

And Lex did

Dear Reader,

I have a confession—my favorite type of heroine to both read and write about is one that may not be all that easy to love at first. She's tough and prickly and pushes people away. Why? Because beneath that prickly exterior is a whole lot of vulnerability. And vulnerability is scary. My heroine, Alexa Benjamin, is such a woman. She was raised by her single bullfighter father and grew up on the rodeo circuit, watching her dad prevent disaster—until he had his own disaster in the form of a heart attack while saving a bull rider. Lex isn't afraid of much...except for losing someone else she loves.

Enter Grady Owen, a bull rider who not only drives Lex crazy with his cocky attitude, but also challenges her on many levels. Lex loves a good challenge and enjoys engaging with Grady...right up until she realizes that her feelings for him are changing, growing deeper, keeping her up at night. She will not allow herself to become involved with someone she may lose, and Grady isn't the kind of guy who's going to give up without a fight. The battle is on.

This is my first Harlequin American Romance book and I'm so thrilled to be part of the line. I write what I know—small towns, cowboys, rodeos and ranches. Harlequin American Romance is the perfect place to do that. I had so much fun writing *The Bull Rider Meets His Match,* and I hope you enjoy reading Lex and Grady's story.

I love hearing from readers. Please feel free to contact me via my website, jeanniewatt.com, or my Facebook page, facebook.com/jeannie.watt.1.

Happy Reading!

Jeannie Watt

THE BULL RIDER
MEETS HIS MATCH

—

JEANNIE WATT

HARLEQUIN® AMERICAN ROMANCE®

Recycling programs
for this product may
not exist in your area.

ISBN-13: 978-0-373-75612-4

The Bull Rider Meets His Match

Printed in U.S.A.

www.Harlequin.com

Jeannie Watt lives in a historic Nevada ranching community with her husband, horses, ponies, dogs and cat. When she's not writing, Jeannie loves to horseback ride, sew vintage fashions and, of course, read romance.

Books by Jeannie Watt

HARLEQUIN SUPERROMANCE

A Cowboy's Redemption
Cowboy Comes Back
Always a Temp
Once and for All
Maddie Inherits a Cowboy
Crossing Nevada

The Brodys of Lightning Creek

To Tempt a Cowgirl
To Kiss a Cowgirl

The Montana Way

Once a Champion
Cowgirl in High Heels
All for a Cowboy

I'd like to dedicate this book to
Kathleen Scheibling, who guided me
through my first Harlequin sale many years ago.
Thank you, Kathleen!
It's good to be working with you again.

Chapter One

Alexa Benjamin had yet to see a bull rider who didn't walk as if he owned the world, and the guy coming up the front walk of her best friend's house? He looked as if he were in charge of the universe. Never in her twenty-eight years had she encountered anyone as sure of himself as Grady Owen. Nor anyone quite as irritating.

Lex stepped back from the window, gave her shoulders a roll then started toward the front door to head off trouble. Grady had just hit the top step when she walked out onto the porch and took a stance. When he saw her, his expression shifted from good-natured to hard so quickly it would have been comical if she didn't suspect that he was there to screw up her best friend's life. Again.

"Lex. What a pleasant surprise." But there was no hint of friendliness in his gray eyes.

"Same here," she said, folding her arms over her chest as she studied the man who was not going to get into the house. Like all bull riders, Grady was one tightly packed unit: average height, lean and wiry. Lex knew if she reached out and ran a hand over his arm, or any part of his body for that matter, all she would feel would be sinew and muscle. Sometimes, in the past, she'd felt a subtle urge to do just that, to touch his fascinatingly hard body. But Grady had always had that effect on her. He drove her crazy with his self-absorbed attitude and cockiness, yet a small part of her found him interesting. She'd reminded herself on more than one occasion that some people found major disasters interesting, also.

She raised her chin. "What can I do for you?"

He tipped back his ball cap, giving her a glimpse of the faint scar that crossed his forehead just below his hairline. "I'm here to see Danielle."

Lex brushed back a few strands of dark hair that the breeze had blown across her face. The rest was still caught in the silver barrette her father had made her shortly before he died.

"Danielle is busy. Up to her neck in wedding plans." She felt a touch of mean satisfaction. Her friend was marrying a guy who put *her* first instead of his career. Grady had done the exact opposite.

"So I hear." He shifted his weight and crossed his arms, mirroring her pose as he eyed her up and down, his gaze challenging. Fine. Bring it on. Lex loved nothing more than a good challenge. "And you're still her watchdog?"

"I'm her friend." Lex spoke lightly, but there was an edge of steel in her voice.

"I just want to talk to her."

"But you don't have to talk now."

"What's wrong with now?"

"Here's what's wrong with now," she said, pointing a finger at him. "Her mom, her grandma and her great-grandma are in the kitchen with her, going over photos of their weddings. I am not going to have you, the former fiancé, busting in and upsetting any of them." Danielle's grandma, Lorraine Perry, was the closest thing Lex had ever had to a grandma of her own, and she would not see her upset. Or Danielle, or her mother, Mae. Great-granny...Great-granny could probably take care of Grady on her own, and if he persisted in hanging around, Lex might just call her out here.

"I understand." But he didn't move. He had that stubborn bull rider expression on his face. That "the odds are against me but I will prevail" look. "If you give me her phone number, I'll call her and set up a time."

Lex couldn't help smirking at him. "I don't think so."

Grady looked over her shoulder as if willing Danielle to come to the door and see what was going on. When he looked back at Lex, his expression was once again hard, his gray eyes deadly. "What happens between me and Danielle is none of your business. It isn't now, and it wasn't back then."

Lex merely tilted her head, unimpressed. "I know a train wreck when I see it coming. You have train wreck written all over you."

"And you have controlling…"

"Bitch written all over me?" she asked smoothly, daring him to agree out loud.

"Your words. Not mine."

"I bet." He wasn't all that close, but as the breeze wafted over them, his scent hit her nostrils—soap and guy and maybe some kind of aftershave—and it made her once again conscious of him in ways she'd rather not be. It was an unsettling feeling, this odd prickle of awareness that seemed to come out of nowhere. Especially when he was looking at her so coldly.

"I'm going to see Danielle."

"I'm sure you are," she said. "But it's not going to be right now."

Grady's mouth flattened even more as he cocked a speculative eyebrow at her. "Good talking to you, Lex." He turned and marched down the bumpy walk to the gate, and Lex decided it was too much to hope that he tripped over one of the concrete edges pushed up by tree roots.

Not a very charitable thought, but Grady Owen had turned Danielle's life inside out only a few years before, and while Lex knew that her friend could fight her own fights, she saw no reason for her to do so. Not when she was there to do it for her.

Grady's classic Ford F-250 roared to life—literally roared, thanks to the straight exhaust pipes—and he wheeled the truck in a circle then pulled out of the driveway. Only then did Lex go back into the house.

"Was that UPS?" Danielle called, poking her blond head out of the kitchen. Her normally serene expression was a bit frazzled, and Lex was glad she'd sent Grady on his way. Wedding plans were stressful enough without the former fiancé being involved.

"Just a guy who was lost and needed some directions," Lex said as she followed her friend into the cozy kitchen and took her place at the table strewn with wedding photos. She'd fess up to Danielle later, but right now she wanted to get back to the business of deciding whose wedding dress would best be altered to fit Danielle on her big day. In her opinion, none of the vintage dresses would work, but it was up to Danielle to either pick one or tell her mom and grandmother and great-grandmother *no, thanks*. It was Lex's job to pour the wine after the task was done.

GRADY PULLED UP to his sister's house and parked the truck behind the wind-damaged barn. He stepped over a few boards as he got out of the truck, thankful that Annie and the girls were still out grocery shopping. He'd yet to shake the black mood brought on by dealing with the she-devil. Who did Lex Benjamin think she was? He was pretty certain that Danielle wouldn't have broken their engagement if it hadn't been for Lex. They would have had troubles in the beginning, no doubt. All married couples did, but they would have worked them out. Thanks to Ms. Benjamin, they never had a chance. She'd been against their relationship from day one and had never been shy about saying so.

He walked into the kitchen and hung his hat on one of the pegs by the door, only to have the peg fall off the wall. His hat hit the floor at his feet and the peg rolled across the worn tiles, stopping under his mom's antique maple table.

Even though his sister had a way with paint and bright accents, there was no getting around the fact that their childhood home was in deep need of a monetary infusion. The place had been run-down when Annie moved in, and even though she'd made it look cheery, nothing had been done to fix the real problems—leaky windows, worn flooring, aging plumbing.

Grady picked up his hat and the peg, setting both on the counter as he tried to remember where he'd last seen the wood glue. The cellar? He started down the steps, not liking the way they sagged and creaked beneath his weight. He'd only been home for two days, but he already felt as if he'd made a mistake spending his winters practicing and working in Oklahoma. He should have hung closer to home, taking care of matters such as loose pegs and saggy steps.

And relationships.

Yeah. Relationships.

Maybe if he'd taken one season off, given Danielle time to get used to his career, things would have worked out between them. But he hadn't been able to make that sacrifice.

Stupid move.

And Lex. She'd been against their relationship from the beginning, and Danielle had listened to her. They'd been close friends for as long as he could remember, which had always struck him as odd because the two women were polar opposites. Danielle was fair—blond haired, blue-eyed—sweet, accommodating. Lex had a mass of dark hair and hazel eyes and she was in no way sweet or accommodating. She was hard. Brittle almost. But that mouth…he had to admit to being fascinated by those soft, full lips that seemed to be in a permanent pout whenever she was concentrating on something other than taking him out.

Grady reached for the cord to turn on the overhead light as he stepped onto the stone floor.

Shelves of home canning and dry goods lined both sides of the rock-walled space. At the far wall, a couple of old bureaus stood on either side of the hot water heater, and Grady crossed to them, opening drawers until he found one loaded with string, coils of wire and a few basic hand tools. An ancient bottle of wood glue lay on its side.

He started back up the creaky stairs with the bottle. Another project he'd tackle before he left.

After gluing the peg back in place and checking to see if the others needed reinforcing, Grady opened the fridge and pulled out a beer, then put it back and closed the door again. His stomach was still in a knot, and beer wasn't going to change that. Hammering might, though, so he changed into his work clothes. He planned to head over to Hennessey's ranch to take a look at the practice bulls later that afternoon, but he had time to knock some of the damaged wood off the frame of the barn before he left.

His sister had really had an odd run of luck over the past few months. The company where she'd worked for five years folded, and while she'd found a part-time job, she still hadn't found a full-time position that paid well enough to support her small family. The cows she'd hoped to sell to tide her over had come down with an ailment that required quarantine, and then, to top things off, a freak tornado had torn through the area, knocking down hundred-year-old trees and damaging only two buildings in the entire valley— Annie's garage and small barn. That was when his sister had started to crumble, and Grady knew he had to come home.

He and Annie owned the place outright and hadn't insured the buildings for replacement value, so he was the one doing the rebuilding and watching the girls while Annie went to work part-time at the library. He had a feeling that babysitting was going to be more of a workout than riding practice bulls. The girls took after him, it seemed. Lots of energy and lots of ideas.

Despite his dark mood, he smiled as he grabbed

his work gloves. He didn't want to see his nieces become bull riders—too much risk—but he was going to see to it that they got a proper foundation in whatever they chose to funnel all that energy into. Annie and the girls were all he had right now, and he was going to make certain their lives were good.

DANIELLE GATHERED UP delicate floral teacups—she'd gotten out the good china for her wedding gown summit—and carefully hand-washed them while Lex studied the photos on the table. The five women had not come to a consensus as to which wedding dress could best be altered for the ceremony, and Lex wasn't certain they ever would.

"The 1980s is out." She pushed the photo aside.

"Agreed," Danielle said with feeling.

"Which one do *you* like?" Lex asked. Danielle had spent most of the meeting pointing out the merits of each dress and trying not to hurt feelings, so Lex had no idea what she was really thinking. Danielle excelled at tact.

"I like Great-granny's, but she's smaller than me and I don't think it'll work." Great-granny's was the best of the group. Designed in the mid-1940s, when fabric rationing had still been in effect, it was made of heavy satin, with a narrow skirt, a sweetheart neckline and broad shoulders that could be altered fairly easily. Or so Danielle said. Lex knew little about sewing.

"Which leaves mid-1960s." Lex shrugged. "It's not a bad dress." It had a waistline and full skirt. Lots of lace and satin…but it wasn't the right kind of dress for Danielle, who was toned and leggy and needed a simpler body-skimming dress.

Danielle wiped her hands on an embroidered towel. "How am I going to tell them that I want my own gown?"

"By taking a deep breath and blurting out the words?"

Danielle nodded and sat at the table, idly picking up the photo of the 1980s dress. "Mom was beautiful, even if the shoulders on this dress make her look as if she's about to go out for a pass."

"I see no way you could alter this dress and have any of it left."

"Pretty much I would rip the sleeves off."

"And the butt ruffle?"

"Definitely out." Danielle set down a photo and met Lex's gaze. "Who was at the door earlier?"

There was no sense hedging. "Grady."

"I thought so. I recognized the sound of the truck. Did he tell you what he wanted?"

"To see you. Sorry if I overstepped by sending him on his way. I didn't want to upset anyone."

"No. I'm glad you did." An unreadable look flickered across Danielle's face, followed by a sigh. "I guess I need to see him before he hits the road again."

"You don't *have* to."

"I did break up with him over the phone." And she'd made the right choice, but that hadn't kept her from feeling bad for weeks afterward. He'd chosen rodeo over her. Hard to forgive that, but Danielle was the forgiving sort. Far more so than Lex.

"You owe him nothing."

"I know," Danielle said simply.

There was a lot more Lex wanted to say on the subject, but why? When push came to shove, it wasn't her business—even though she never wanted to see Danielle that unhappy again. Ever.

"I need to get home," she said. "The menagerie will be hungry." She stood and picked up her rhinestone-studded leather bag—one of the top sellers at their Western-themed store, Annie Get Your Gun. "I'll see you tomorrow morning."

They met every Wednesday to discuss business, drink tea and share any gossip that Danielle picked up from her grandmother, who owned the building where their boutique was located. But all the gossip had already been passed along during the wedding dress summit, so the meeting would be all business tomorrow.

"Great. I'm looking forward to some nonwedding talk."

"That works for me." Lex gave the photos one last look, then met Danielle's eyes. "Be strong." She was talking about both wedding gowns and ex-fiancés.

"Always."

Lex certainly hoped so.

Chapter Two

Lex tried not to worry about Danielle on the drive home, but the Owen Farm was halfway between her place and Danielle's, so it was hard not to worry when she drove by and caught sight of Grady's truck parked behind the wind-damaged barn. He'd been driving that same truck since high school—not that he'd been home to drive it even once during the past two years. It was as if after Danielle had given him his walking orders, he'd given up on Gavin, Montana, and the people there.

She pulled into her long driveway, smiled as the horses, knowing that they were about to be fed, cantered across the pasture. She loved her ranch, hated that she was now on it alone. But it wasn't being alone that bothered her—it was the fact that her father was never coming back that ruined her. It'd been just her and her dad for so long that it was still hard to accept that he wasn't there.

During the school year, when he'd been on the bull-riding circuit fighting bulls, doing his best to keep a half-ton animal from stomping the cowboy that had just ridden him, she'd often stayed with Danielle's family. After Lex hit high school, she became the farm-sitter during the school year. When summer came, she'd traveled with her dad. By necessity, the father-daughter trips had become fewer and farther between after she'd gotten her first real job, but as luck would have it, she had been there for the final trip. The one when he'd died in the arena—not from a bull injury, but from a heart attack after saving a guy who'd been hung up in the rigging and beaten like a rag doll as the bull attempted to knock him free.

Even now, years later, the memory made her tear up—especially if it came at a time when she was worried about something else, such as, say, a close friend who was too nice for her own good. Lex blinked hard a few times before parking her truck next to her dad's. She had two precious reminders of her father on the ranch that she refused to get rid of—his truck and his rank old horse, Snuff.

Three dogs bounded out from behind the house when she got out of the truck, two border collies and a rambunctious dusty brown terrier that'd shown up on the ranch and refused to leave. A small black-and-white cat trotted behind the dogs. Felicity was another orphan, found abandoned at the county dump before her eyes were open.

"Hey, gang," Lex said as she closed the truck door. The dogs professed great joy at her return, while Felicity stood back, waiting for Lex to scoop her up on her way into the house. Once there, she shed her town clothes and climbed into a pair of well-worn jeans and a sweatshirt. She popped a John Deere ball cap on her head, grabbed her least offensive pair of gloves out of the basket by the door and headed back out the door to feed.

Somehow she had collected way too many animals

after her father died, but she didn't have the heart to let any of them go. It wasn't as if she couldn't afford to feed them. Her father had left her the ranch in excellent shape financially and he'd had life insurance, which she'd invested. Lex was pretty much set for life, as long as she managed the property in a sensible manner, and since she was all about sensible, that wasn't a problem. She started across the gravel drive leading to the barn and was met halfway by two Mediterranean donkeys, which brayed at her, and a pygmy goat that bumped the back of her legs as she walked.

Okay, maybe she wasn't totally sensible, but everyone had their foibles.

Followed by her entourage, Lex tossed hay, dumped grain, checked water troughs. The donkeys and goat abandoned her once they had their rations, but Felicity and the dogs—Pepper, Ginger and little brown Dave the Terror—stayed close to her throughout the daily routine. Once she got back to the house, she held the door open. The dogs raced in and Felicity turned and walked across the porch to a spot in the sun.

Lex understood. An independent woman could only take so much social interaction before welcoming time to herself. She was the same way, although lately the house seemed a little too lonely. It was the anniversary, she told herself as she changed back out of her feeding clothes and pulled a loose cotton dress over her head. Two years since she'd watched her father collapse onto the dirt of the arena, clutching his chest.

Last year she'd told herself that the pain would ease by the time the next anniversary rolled around, and it had, but not as much as she'd hoped. It hurt to be alone and it hurt to know she'd never again hear her father's boots crossing the front porch as he returned from a trip.

In that regard, alone sucked.

GRADY WAS JUST putting the finishing touches on dinner when a car pulled into the drive. It wasn't until it parked in front of the house instead of near the barn that he realized it wasn't Annie and her girls returning from the big shopping trip in Bozeman. He didn't recognize the car, but he definitely recognized the blond getting out of it. Danielle. Tall, cool, beautiful, just as he remembered her.

He pulled the dish towel off his shoulder and dropped it on the kitchen table on his way to the door, glad once again that his sister and nieces were late getting home.

Danielle smiled up at him as he opened the door, but it wasn't the bright open smile he was used to. No. There was a definite touch of wariness in her expression, amplified by the taut way she held her body. Granted, two years had passed since he'd last seen her, but he was surprised at how unfamiliar she seemed, while his encounter with Lex had been like old times. Bad old times.

"Something smells good," she said instead of hello.

"My famous pot roast." He stepped back, silently inviting her into Annie's cozy kitchen. She came inside, and he closed the door. Then for two or three silent seconds they simply stood, like two complete strangers that unexpectedly found themselves sharing a small space. Danielle cleared her throat and met his gaze.

"Lex said you came by today."

He hadn't expected that. He'd figured Lex would do

her best to shield her friend from the evilness that was him and never mention his visit. "I did. She said you and your grandmas were busy talking wedding plans."

She gave a slow nod. "That's true."

"Good guy?"

"The best." She spoke with conviction. "I'm engaged. I'm happy."

"And you don't want me to mess things up."

An expression of relief crossed her face as he said what was obviously on her mind. "In a nutshell, yes."

Fair enough. When she'd broken up with him, over the phone, since he'd been in the middle of his season and she'd apparently taken all she could take, she sounded torn, as if she wasn't entirely certain she was doing the right thing. But now…now she looked like a woman who knew her mind.

"I won't mess up your life."

"Thank you. I didn't know if you'd come to see me—" her expression shifted to a tentative one "—with thoughts of us getting together again."

"The thought might have crossed my mind." It definitely had. He'd wondered more than once if they might now be in a place where they could reevaluate their relationship…maybe even pick it up again.

She gave him a suspicious look. "Might have?"

"Well, I hadn't seen you in a while, but I thought about you a lot. I wondered…you know…" He gave a small shrug. "I wanted to see you one more time. To make sure."

"And now?"

It was funny how standing here in this kitchen with Danielle, the flesh and blood Danielle, not the Danielle in his memories, made things so much clearer. He felt no strong urge to take her in his arms, hold her close, ask if it was too late. "I'm happy for you."

Her expression cleared at the sincerity in his voice. "Thank you." She reached out to gently touch his shoulder. "We were never meant to be, Grady."

"What if I hadn't ridden bulls?" A small part of him had to know if it had been the bulls.

"Ultimately...I don't think it would have mattered."

"I think you're right." He'd thought he loved her, but he hadn't been able to sacrifice for her. "We had some good times."

"We had some excellent times. You taught me a thing or two about taking risks." Danielle smiled at him, the old smile he remembered so well. "If you're comfortable with it, I'll send you a wedding invitation."

"I'd like that. Thanks." He realized then that it felt totally right for him to be in the audience instead of at the altar on Danielle's wedding day. He had an affection for her, deep respect for her, but he knew in his gut they didn't belong together.

After she drove away, Grady went back to the gravy simmering on top of the stove and gave it a stir. Strange how things worked out. For two years he'd essentially stopped dating. He'd used Danielle as the standard by which he'd measured all women, and no one had measured up.

And now it seemed that his standard had been something he'd worked up in his head, not the woman he'd once thought he'd loved.

ANNIE GET YOUR GUN smelled of potpourri, spices and flowers, and Lex always inhaled deeply as she walked into the homey space she and Danielle had worked so hard to create after she'd lost her father and Danielle broke up with Grady. She loved this place.

On the far wall was a framed poster of Annie Oakley with her rifle, embellished with paint and glitter. The store itself was filled with quirky Western-themed decor items as well as personal accessories, books, jewelry, T-shirts and fun gift ideas. Most of the stuff they purchased outright, but they had consignment stock—antiques and small furniture items—as well as items that Danielle and Lex made themselves. Lex's father had been a silversmith, and Lex used his tools to create funky metal jewelry accented with beads and gemstones. Danielle made one-of-a-kind collector's quilts, and Kelly, their one employee, was a potter.

"Is that you, Lex?" Danielle's voice came from the back room, where they kept extra stock as well as a refrigerator and electric teakettle.

"Yep. I got the scones." She shook the white bag. The pleasant aroma of the cinnamon tea Danielle always made for their weekly business meetings wafted from the back room. She set the bag on the antique table they used for their conferences and sat down.

"Kelly won't be here for the meeting," Danielle said as she came out of the back room carrying a tray with the teapot and cups. She smiled tightly as she approached, the picture of stress, and Lex's first thought was, What did Grady do now? She'd had a feeling that Danielle would contact him after she left, just to finish unfinished business. She kept her mouth shut, though, as Danielle set down the tray and opened the bag of scones to arrange them on a porcelain plate embellished with small cowboy boots. When she finished pouring the tea, she finally met Lex's gaze.

"You look like you could use a shot of whiskey in your tea," Lex said.

Danielle waved her hand dismissively. "I told my mom and grandmas that I was going to buy my own dress this morning. I hate disappointing any of them."

Okay. At least it wasn't Grady that was bothering her. And as for Danielle buying her own dress, it had to be done. That '80s dress…

"I have a feeling," Lex said, raising her cup, "that your mom might have disappointed her mom, who in turn disappointed Great-granny, since they all have their own dresses."

"Good point." Danielle frowned and then said, "Great point. Anyway, now I'm going to be gown shopping, and I was hoping you might be able to squeeze some time in to help me."

"As long as it's not Saturday morning, I'm at your disposal."

"Big plans?"

"I promised Jared I'd bring quiet horses to the Kids' Club riding lessons that start this weekend." Her only cousin, a single dad, worked long hours in a machine shop during the week and then volunteered for the local recreation program on his weekends. "After all the help he gave me after Dad died, I figured it was the least I could do."

"Are you helping with lessons?"

"Just providing mounts. Jared has high school kids helping with lessons." Lex frowned at Danielle. "Where is Kelly?" Who was the kind of person who never missed work, never missed a meeting.

Danielle's mouth flattened as she said, "Job interview."

Lex set her cup back on the saucer. "No."

"Afraid so. County courthouse. Primo benefits."

"Wow." They paid Kelly fairly well but weren't in a position to offer anything better than bare-bones benefits. "What now?"

"She'll know tomorrow if she gets the job and has promised to do everything she can to help us find someone."

"I don't think we can find someone like her." Kelly made every customer feel special, even the crotchety ones like Mrs. Lacombe, who came to browse and complain about prices at least once a week.

"I know," Danielle said wearily, "but we have to think about what's best for Kelly."

OF COURSE KELLY got the job. Danielle called later in the afternoon to break the news to Lex, who was just heading out to feed.

"I can help out at the store until we get someone." Lex loved stocking the store and guiding the business decisions, but she wasn't the warm and fuzzy people person that Kelly and Danielle were. She'd been in deep mourning for her father when she and Danielle started the business, and because of that, Danielle had taken charge of the day-to-day operations. She also pulled in a larger percentage of the proceeds. It worked well. Danielle had more income and Lex had the time she needed to focus on her farm.

"I have an idea," Danielle said slowly. "What do you think of interviewing Annie Owen?"

"Annie Owen?" Lex barely kept herself from saying, *Are you nuts?* Instead she said, "Why Annie?"

"Her name is perfect. Annie?" Lex rolled her eyes and waited for the real reason. "We know her. She needs a full-time job. It would help her and it would help us."

And also bring Grady, Annie's brother, firmly back into Danielle's sphere.

"But," Danielle said, "if you have a problem with hiring her, I won't call."

Lex could almost hear her dad saying, *Step back*, as he often did when Lex felt the urge to fix matters that weren't necessarily her concern. She liked Annie Owen, had nothing against her, except for her brother. And honestly, the only thing she had against *him* was that he'd been utterly selfish in regards to her friend.

Let things play out. Stop trying to save everyone.

Fine. She'd back off...but that didn't mean she wouldn't remain vigilant. She smiled at Danielle and gave a dismissive shrug. "If you're good with it, I'm good with it."

"If you're concerned about me and Grady, don't be. I went to see him."

"I figured you would."

"Yes. And I felt...nothing." Danielle gave a small shrug. "I'd bet the store that Grady felt the same."

"Well...that's good news." Very good news. No more worrying about her friend getting mixed up with a selfish bull rider.

"It is. And now there's no reason not to hire Annie."

Lex gave a slow nod. "I agree."

"Great. I'll see if she wants to meet us at the store tomorrow."

"ARE YOU SURE about this?" Annie asked, casting Grady a concerned look as she wrapped a blue silk scarf loosely around her neck.

All of her looks seemed to be concerned lately. Stress had taken a toll on his sister. She didn't smile as much as she used to, didn't seem to feel as bullet-proof. She was dressed for her interview in clothes that Grady recognized, and he hadn't been home for two years, which made him wonder if he should have pressed harder for her to take the money he'd offered her. Annie had her pride, but there came a point where accepting monetary help was a matter of common sense. The house needed work, she needed some new clothes and there were her two young daughters to care for.

"I'm sure," Grady said with an easy grin.

"Emily offered to take care of them." Emily Mansanti was the girls' usual afternoon babysitter, who'd happened to have a free morning today.

"Why spend the money when you have me?" He wasn't fool enough to add, "How hard could it be to take care of two little girls?" The past several days had taught him exactly how hard it could be. Kristen and Katie put new meaning into the word *energetic*. Although they were blond-haired-green-eyed images of their sensible brown-haired, blue-eyed mother, they seemed to have inherited their uncle Grady's sense of adventure. And now he was getting an idea of the challenges he must have presented his own parents. Constant energy was exhausting.

Annie gave her head a small shake. "Just making sure," she said as the girls walked into the kitchen.

"Good luck on your job," Kristen said, hugging Annie around the waist.

"I don't have it yet, sweetie, but I'm going to give it a shot."

"We still get to go to riding lessons, right?" Katie piped up. "If you get the job."

"I'm going to take you to lessons," Grady said.

Before the girls could respond, Annie said, "He'll take you to lessons *if* you behave while I'm gone. If you don't…" She held up a finger in a warning gesture, and both girls nodded solemnly.

Somewhere along the line Annie had shifted from easygoing sister to strict mom.

"You're going to be late," Grady said.

"Yeah. Wish me luck."

"Good luck," Grady said. He'd told himself a couple of times that morning that they wouldn't have called her in for an interview if she wasn't a serious candidate. He didn't trust Lex, but he did trust Danielle, and the fact that she'd arranged for the interview *after* they talked made him feel hopeful for his sister's chances. Heaven knew she was due for a break.

"Do we get to help you build the garage?" Kristen asked as soon as the door shut behind her mother.

"Please?" Katie asked. "We like to hammer."

"Yeah," Grady said. In fact, that sounded like a fine idea. They could hammer nails into a board and he could get some work done on the frame. He found two lightweight tack hammers in the tool box and two sturdy boards. After partially hammering ten nails into each board, he cautioned the girls to grip the hammer with both hands and to *never* hold the nails with their fingers. He also told them to tap, not wallop.

Maybe he'd given a few too many strict instructions because after ten minutes, the girls became bored with mindless hammering and wanted another job. It didn't take long for him to realize that he wasn't going to get a lot done while they were there helping him.

"What else can you guys do while I work?" he asked. An idea struck him. "Hey, shouldn't you be reading books for that library award thing your mom told me about?" After the twins had gone to bed the previous evening, Annie had explained to Grady that her girls were dead set on winning the local library's Dedicated Reader Awards. It was a big deal in town, and part of Grady's duties would be to sign off on their reading sheets and take them to the library when they ran low on books.

"We finished our books last night," Kristen said. "Mom's picking up more today."

"Um…" Katie frowned a little. "We could clean our rooms."

Grady lifted a skeptical eyebrow. No kids he knew of volunteered to clean their rooms. "What's the catch?"

"It's almost time for allowance and if our rooms aren't clean, we don't get allowance."

Annie really had become a hard-ass. But she always had been a neat freak, so Grady understood the clean-rooms-linked-to-allowance thing.

"Cool." They'd clean their rooms, get their allowance and he'd get some framing done. Win-win. "If you're done by lunch and do a good job, I'll add extra money to your allowance."

The girls exchanged excited glances, then started running toward the house, laughing as they went.

Feeling rather smug, Grady went back to framing. He figured it was almost two hours until lunch. The girls would probably start cleaning their rooms, then segue into a session of cartoon streaming as they'd done the previous evening while he and Annie discussed futures—hers and his. His sister was struggling, but she wasn't giving up. He was somehow going to help her without making her feel beholden. Neat trick, that, but he'd figure it out. In the meantime, he would rebuild the garage, patch the barn and re-inforce the cellar stairs. He owned half the property, and it was only right that he help with the upkeep, de-spite Annie pointing out that he didn't live there so he didn't reap any benefits. He was reaping them now.

Grady lost himself in the building process as the sun climbed in the sky. He glanced at his watch and realized almost two hours had passed since the girls went inside. He was hungry and thirsty, and he imag-ined the girls were probably also in need of lunch.

He pulled his ball cap off as he approached the house and slapped it on his thigh. Annie had made sun tea the day before, and he needed about a gallon of it right now. He pushed open the back door into the kitchen and then stopped dead in his tracks as his boots hit a puddle and two pairs of startled green eyes connected with his.

"What the—" He barely cut off the curse. Swallow-ing hard, he stepped over the wide puddle of tea and broken glass. "Hey! Don't touch the glass," he yelled as Katie started picking up the pieces with her bare hands. She instantly dropped the shards and stepped back, putting her hands behind her. Grady walked through the mess and took her hands in his, examining them closely. Other than being sticky from something chocolaty, they seemed fine.

"All right," he said once he was satisfied he wouldn't be rendering first aid. "How did this hap…" The word trailed off as he suddenly became aware of the condition of the rest of the kitchen, which had been close to spotless when Annie had left. *Egad.* Where had all that chocolate come from?

He shifted his gaze back to his nieces, unable to find words. They seemed similarly afflicted until Kristen blinked at him, all wide green eyes and stricken expression. "We wanted to surprise you with a cake."

Chapter Three

Indeed, there were signs of cake making in the form of chocolate batter pretty much everywhere, including the front of the fridge, the cabinets and the floor. No fewer than five bowls were stacked in the sink, along with a gooey eggbeater lying on the counter. Grady picked it up gingerly and set it in the bowls.

"We aren't allowed to use the mixer," Katie explained, casually wiping her gooey hands down the sides of her pink jeans.

Grady could only imagine the havoc they could have created with an electric mixer tossing batter around the room. "I see." He rubbed his jaw as he took in the carnage. If he was quick, there was an off chance they could get the mess cleaned up before Annie got home.

"Here's the deal, guys. I want you to stay out of here until I get the floor cleaned up, then—"

The sound of a car interrupted his words.

"Mom," the girls said simultaneously in a hushed tone.

"Sounds like it," he agreed, heading for the door and shooting a look out the window. It was indeed Annie who'd pulled into the drive. He turned back to the two wide-eyed girls. "Why don't you two wait in the living room?"

They turned without argument and walked side by side down the hall. Katie had a perfect chocolate handprint on her backside. They'd just disappeared into the living room when he heard Kristen say in a low voice, "She's going to be mad."

No doubt.

Grady pulled open the door to take the heat.

Annie practically danced up the sidewalk. "I got the job!"

"Congratulations," Grady said, forcing a quick smile. He glanced over his shoulder at the house.

"What happened?" Annie's voice instantly went flat. The Mom Voice.

"Well…" Grady shrugged. "Slight mishap. The ice tea jug got knocked out of the fridge and broke."

Annie paled. "No one got hurt?"

"No." That was the good news. "But the mess is still there."

"It happens," Annie said as she headed past him to the door.

"And the girls made a cake."

She stopped dead and turned back to him. "With supervision…right?"

He gave a small cough. "It was kind of an independent project."

A curse slipped out of Annie's lips followed by an even more colorful curse when she opened the door. For a moment she simply stood cataloging the damage to her kitchen. "Did they ask?"

"Uh…"

"Answer enough. Where are they?"

"Living room."

She carefully skirted the broken glass in her heels before marching toward the living room. Grady thought about intervening, since he had vague memories of him and Annie doing the exact same thing, minus the broken tea jug, but decided not to risk the wrath of his sister.

Half an hour later the kitchen was cleaned, the girls fed and playing on their swing set and Grady was waiting to hear that he was an irresponsible uncle. Instead Annie opened the fridge and looked inside. "Good. Beer. Do you want one?"

Annie didn't normally partake at home, and Grady hated the thought that he'd driven her to drink. "Sure."

She pulled out two bottles and set them on the counter. He automatically stepped over to open them and then handed one to Annie before touching the top of his bottle to hers. "Congratulations, sis. I wish your homecoming had been better."

"Yes. That's what I want to talk to you about." She held the bottle in front of her but had yet to take a sip. "I have a favor to ask."

"Yeah?" he asked cautiously.

"I know you plan to practice at Hennessey's while you're here, and you're going to be busy with the garage and barn and I know today was a bit of a disaster, but—" she pressed her lips together "—could you also watch the girls in the mornings? They have their regular sitter for the afternoons, but she can't do mornings."

Grady shrugged as if watching the twins were the easiest thing in the world. "Sure. Not a problem."

Annie's face broke into a wide smile. "I don't know about that, but it would really help me out."

"Like I said, not a problem. I came home to help."

"You came home to rebuild the garage and barn, since I underinsured the outbuildings."

"*We* underinsured the outbuildings." Grady went to sit at the kitchen table, but Annie stayed where she was, leaning against the newly cleaned counter. "I don't mind watching the girls. I learned a lot today, and I can't see this—" he gestured at the kitchen "—happening again."

"They'll think of something else," Annie said matter-of-factly. "It's not an easy job keeping them out of trouble."

"I can handle it." He hoped. "I'd even keep them in the afternoons if you want."

"I need to keep my sitter booked or I'll lose her during the school year." And she couldn't count on him then, because he was leaving for a few months at the end of the summer to take part in the traveling Bull Extravaganza Buck-Off.

"Yeah. That makes sense." He grinned at her. It'd been a while since he saw Annie so happy. "I'm glad that you got the job."

"I think I'm going to like it. A lot." She shot him a sideways look after taking a sip of her beer. "Does it bother you that Danielle's getting married?"

"I thought it might, but it doesn't."

She regarded him for a moment, using her truth-detector look. The same look she'd used whenever he said things like, *Honest, I haven't said a word to Joey Barton about you having a crush on him.*

"You sound pretty sure about that," Annie said. "What changed 'it might' to 'it doesn't'?"

"She stopped by and we talked. It's pretty clear to

me now that when I left two years ago, I accidentally did the best thing for both of us."

"So you have no issue with me working for her?"

"Of course not." Actually, he had more of an issue with her working for Lex, but she was a silent partner, as he understood it, so really he had no issue at all. All he wanted was for his sister to be employed and secure.

ANNIE OWEN'S FIRST day of work was a typical summer Monday at the store. Crotchety Mrs. Lacombe stopped by before lunch to admire the quilts and complain bitterly about the prices, even though she was perhaps the wealthiest person in town. Annie did her best to assist the woman, but nothing she did was right. Lex wanted to rescue her, but when you worked in retail, you had to learn to deal with the Mrs. Lacombes of the world. Annie looked as if her smile were literally frozen in place by the time the woman left—empty-handed as usual, a broken salesperson in her wake.

She was barely out the door when four ladies in their midfifties, wearing Yellowstone National Park T-shirts, came in and started oohing and aahing over the Western-themed memorabilia. And, thankfully, they were buyers, so Annie came away from her second retail encounter feeling a lot better about her sales abilities.

"I've never really spoken to Mrs. Lacombe before," Annie said after the Yellowstone women went on their way, each carrying a paper shopping bag filled with gifts for children and grandchildren. "Now I know why," she added with feeling.

Lex fought a smile. She hadn't expected Annie to be so candid. She liked it.

"Mrs. Lacombe can be trying," Lex agreed as she opened the small refrigerator and pulled out the salad and sandwiches she'd brought for lunch. Annie had been given strict instructions not to bring lunch the first day. "Danielle doesn't like it when I help her, because there's usually smoke rolling off my back by the time she leaves but I haven't blown yet."

"Does she ever buy anything?" Annie asked as Danielle came into the workroom.

Lex and Danielle exchanged thoughtful glances. "I think I sold her a set of pot holders once," Lex said. "Right after we opened."

"And I sold her a vase," Danielle said. "The one we'd marked down so many times that if we'd marked it down again, we would have had to pay the person who took it."

Annie laughed. "So she only comes in to browse."

"And browbeat," Lex added with a small grimace. "She's lonely, so we kind of…endure." An odd expression crossed Annie's face, as if she hadn't expected Lex to say something insightful. Or sensitive. Which made her wonder what Grady had said about her.

It didn't matter.

The lunch hour was devoid of customers, so the three women were able to eat without interruption. Danielle did point out that normally they considered that a bad thing. "We've had a good spring and early summer, though," she said, "so this is nice."

The words were barely out of her mouth when the back door opened and Great-granny came in, wearing immaculate jeans and a neatly pressed red gingham Western shirt. She peeked through the workroom door into the shop. "Good. We're alone."

"What's up?" Danielle asked.

"I have a color question." Great-granny pulled a handful of hardware store paint color cards out of her purse and started arranging them on the table in front of Danielle as if she were dealing out a game of solitaire. "I've been looking at bridesmaid dresses. When you say pink, which part of the spectrum are you aiming at?" She laid down the last card and stood back, hands on her narrow hips.

"Well," Danielle said, briefly meeting Lex's gaze before lowering it to the sea of pink in front of her, "I'm not certain, so that is a very good question." She studied the paint chips—Great-granny had the whole range here, from rose to coral, petal to shocking. "Wow. Um…"

There was a knock on the back door then, and Lex tore herself away from the pink debate to answer it, finding herself face-to-face with Grady Owen once she pulled the door open. Her heart shouldn't have jumped, but it did. She was that used to expecting disaster whenever Grady was around.

"Uh, hi," he said, having the good grace to look uncomfortable for once in his life. "I didn't want to call my sister at work, but if she has a moment, we have a slight emergency. I need her advice."

"Never a problem," Lex said coolly, tearing her gaze away from his rather mesmerizing one. She and Danielle knew their employees had lives. She only wished that didn't have to include Grady Owen showing up at her back door. "I'll get her."

A few seconds later Annie was at the door talking to her brother. Lex hadn't intended to eavesdrop, but as she cleared plates so that Great-granny could spread out the pink paint chips, she was close enough to hear Annie say, "Tar? No. Prewash will not get tar out of clothing."

"Then I'm buying them new jeans," Grady replied. "What size are they?"

"Grady, you don't need to buy new jeans, and how in the world—"

The bell rang over the customer entrance and Annie started to turn, but Lex put a hand on her arm on her way by. "You deal. I'll get the customer." Annie looked torn, so Lex said, "It's a cute guy. I don't mind."

She had no idea whether the customer was a cute guy or not, but Annie bought the line and continued talking to Grady while Lex went into the shop to greet the three teenagers gathered around the jewelry display. She sold two necklaces and a pair of earrings, and before she got the sale rung up, Annie was back in the shop.

"Everything okay?" Lex asked as she wrapped the jewelry in red tissue and slipped it into a brown bag with a photo of Annie Oakley on the front. Annie nodded as the girls took their purchases and left the store, debating between themselves whether to get ice cream or a hamburger next.

Once they were gone, Annie pushed the hair back from her forehead with one hand. "All I can say is that the house is still standing and no wildlife has been released in the living room today."

"Sounds like a good day," Lex said.

"Yes. In my world that's an excellent day."

GRADY LOVED HIS NIECES. They constantly surprised him, made him laugh, caused him to feel all protective. They also wore him out. After only a few days of babysitting, he realized that when he left for Hennessey's to do his practice ride in the late afternoons, he was more exhausted than he'd been after driving twelve hours and climbing on top of a Brahma, then getting back in the truck and driving again.

Although that wasn't the best example, because after he started making serious money, he flew to most of his events. During his off time, he lived and worked on his friend Hank Fletcher's Oklahoma ranch. It was a job that gave him a decent paycheck and offered him the flexibility he needed to follow the circuit. He'd sent money to his sister, and sometimes she'd even accepted it; but now that he was around her and the girls more, he was kicking himself for sending a check instead of coming back. Two years hadn't seemed like a long time, but it was. He'd missed out on a lot, and Annie, even though she was stubbornly independent—at least until a tornado turned her life around—could have used his help.

He hadn't been thinking about anyone except for himself, and that wasn't good. Now that he knew what was going on, had become a larger part of his nieces' lives, he'd started crafting a plan. He was going back on the circuit, taking part in the traveling Bull Extravaganza in the fall, because that was how he earned his living, but he was no longer stationing himself in Oklahoma during the off-season. He was moving back to Gavin, taking care of his family. So when Hank called to touch base as Grady was driving home from practice, it was the perfect time to break the news to him. Hank had sounded delighted.

"So it worked out with your lady?"

Hank had met Danielle several times, and even though Grady hadn't said anything to him, he must have deduced that Grady had thought of giving his relationship with Danielle one last shot.

"Nothing to work out. She's getting married and the guy ain't me."

"Hey. Sorry to hear that." Hank sounded genuinely shocked.

"I'm okay with it." And he was all for moving on to the next topic. Hank, however, had a few more things to say on the matter.

"You know what this means?"

"Not really." His tone was not encouraging, but Hank didn't get the hint. Hank had never been a hint kind of guy.

"You need to get back out there, man. You haven't seriously dated in how long?"

Long time. Which had been part of why he'd planned to revisit his relationship with Danielle. He'd figured that she had to be a reason he wasn't that wild about any one particular woman. He'd been wrong.

"A while."

"I'll give you this. Danielle is a real looker, but it takes more than good looks to make a relationship, you know. Especially for a guy in your profession."

"So I'm discovering," Grady said facetiously, still trying to keep things light.

"And now that you've figured that out, you know what you need to do?"

Grady knew.

He needed to get back out there. "I'll keep you posted," he said, and even though he spoke wryly, he realized Hank was totally correct. He needed to develop a social life. A local one, since this was where he planned to live from now on.

After hanging up the phone, he dialed Jess Hayward. If anyone was going to get him back into the swing of things locally, it was a Hayward twin. Even if he didn't find someone to hook up with, he needed to get out of the self-imposed isolation in which he'd existed since Danielle broke up with him. Yeah. He needed to meet some women. Have some fun.

Be the Grady Owen he used to be.

DANIELLE AND LEX threw a going away party for Kelly at the Shamrock Pub, two doors down from Annie Get Your Gun, after her last day of work. Curtis, Danielle's fiancé, joined the party after getting off at the bank and soon the four of them were headed to an impromptu dinner. He was the physical opposite of Grady—tall and blond and built like the football player he'd once been. Needless to say, he was also Grady's emotional opposite, being serious and dependable. In other words, he was better suited to Danielle in all respects, and Lex liked him.

After dinner, Danielle and Curtis made their apologies and went home, leaving Kelly and Lex sharing a bowl of molten chocolate cake as a long evening stretched in front of them.

"Are you in any hurry to get home?" Kelly asked as they left the steak house. She pulled the elastic out of her long red hair as she spoke, shaking her head so that the waves spilled around her shoulders. She was obviously getting into party mode and it was only nine o'clock, so Lex shrugged.

"My dogs might worry, but no."

Kelly jerked her head toward the bar on the other side of the parking lot. "One for the road?"

"Sure."

It'd been a while since Lex set foot in Shardlow's and when they walked in, she had an instant flashback to her college days. The place was filled with cowboys and cowgirls. Loud music pulsed over the speakers, accented by the clack of pool balls on the three tables lined up side by side in an alcove. Kelly had to point to a table, since it was hard to hear over the noise.

It was quieter along the wall, and a tall bar guy appeared almost as soon as they were seated, a towel tucked into the front of his Wranglers, a smile on his handsome face. "What can I get you ladies?"

Kelly beamed up at him, and Lex began to understand the reason behind the nightcap. "A draft, please."

"Same." Lex waited until he was gone before meeting Kelly's gaze across the table. "Okay. Spill."

"Not much to spill." She smiled cheekily. "Yet. He's the owner's nephew. Gus Hawkins. Just moved here from Nevada." The drinks arrived, and Kelly started a tab. The barkeep smiled at her, and Lex had to admit that there was some chemistry behind that smile. Kelly leaned closer after he'd left. "Thank you for coming with me. You can see why I didn't want to come here alone."

Indeed she could. Especially with the bar in full swing. This was not the place for a woman hoping to have a few minutes with the attractive barkeep and not be hit on.

"You don't have to stay long," Kelly said. "I know you have things to do tomorrow. I just—" she smiled again "—wanted a taste."

Lex laughed, wondering if she was a bad friend because she was more in the mood for home and bed than partying and was tempted to take Kelly up on her offer of not staying long.

There was a bit of a commotion toward the rear exit then, and she and Kelly glanced over simultaneously to see none other than Grady Owen and two of his high school buddies, the Hayward twins, Ty and Jess, walk in. And then she pretty much lost sight of Grady as the buckle bunnies started swarming the guys. Bull riders attracted women. That was a flat-out fact.

"You know I'm no fan of rodeo guys, but Grady's hot," Kelly murmured, echoing Lex's grudging thoughts. A server happened by the group and handed each of the bull riders a beer off her tray, making Lex wonder if someone else was doing without a drink for the moment. The girl turned around and headed back to the bar. Yes, bull riders got special favors here.

"That appears to be the consensus." Lex couldn't argue with it, either. Grady had killer good looks and he could be charming. Even now she could see the flash of his smile from between a blonde and a redhead.

"I might go join the crowd," Kelly said with a suggestive lift of her eyebrows.

"All you'll do is to make a massive ego even bigger."

Kelly laughed and Grady's gaze came up then, zeroing in on Lex almost as if he'd heard her speak. Which was ridiculous, of course, as was the slight bump in her pulse as he started across the room toward her. A few cowgirls trailed behind him.

"Lex," he said, raising his beer in a salute.

She mimicked his salute, then said, "You know Kelly, right?"

"Yes, ma'am." He flashed a smile at both of them.

Oh, yeah. All country boy charm. She was about to comment, when he said on a note of sincerity, "I want to thank you for hiring my sister. She'll do a good job for you. And thank you for letting me interrupt the other day with my twin emergency."

Lex opened her moth, then closed it again. Nothing like a heartfelt thank-you to stop a potentially snarky conversation. She cleared her throat. "Annie will be a good fit."

Grady smiled. "I was surprised she got the job."

"Well," Lex said, "the name was right." She smiled politely at him, wanting him to leave, wanting to stop feeling this odd awareness that had appeared out of nowhere once he walked into the bar and was surrounded by women. Where had that come from? "I don't want to keep you from your—" somehow she managed to choke back the word *groupies* "—friends."

"Thank you, again," he said, before nodding at Kelly and then heading back across the bar where Ty and Jess were busy flirting and drinking.

When Lex looked back at Kelly, she found her friend frowning at her. "Is it just me, or were there a lot of unspoken messages in that conversation?"

Lex shrugged innocently. "Just you."

"Right."

Lex and Kelly nursed their beers and talked for a good twenty minutes before Kelly's bar guy came back, only he wasn't wearing his towel apron and he was carrying three beers. Lex instantly understood what was going on and raised her eyebrows at Kelly in silent communication.

Kelly gave a smiling nod and Lex said, "I hope that beer's not for me. I have to go."

"I'm sure we can find it a home." The guy held out his hand. "I'm Gus."

"Alexa." Lex shook hands, then got up from her chair. "I'll see you around, Kelly. Good luck with the new job. Nice to meet you, Gus."

"New job?" Gus said as he sat down, and Lex took the opportunity to slip away toward the rear exit leading directly to the parking lot. Cool air hit her face as soon as she stepped out the door onto the gravel. She inhaled deeply, filling her lungs with air that didn't smell of beer and too many bodies in a close place.

"Making it an early night?"

Lex jumped a mile at the unexpected voice not far from her shoulder, then whirled to see that Grady had followed her out the door. "You scared the crap out of me."

"You should be more aware of your surroundings."

He took a step forward and Lex drew herself up. "Walk you to your car?" he asked.

"Truck." She was about to say *no*, then realized that was exactly what he expected her to say and the contrary part of her said, "Sure, why not?"

She could see that she'd surprised him by accepting his offer and decided she liked the feeling. "I'm parked on the other side of Main near the Shamrock."

"Long ways away," he said as they fell into step.

"We started Kelly's going-away party there."

"Ah."

They walked shoulder to shoulder, gravel crunching

beneath their boots. Grady was only a couple of inches taller than her, but somehow he seemed to take over the space around them. He was that kind of guy—a bit overpowering. Lex wasn't about to be overpowered.

"So you're babysitting while Annie is at work."

He smiled, shaking his head.

"Not anymore?" Had the tar incident done him in?

"Yes. I'm the sitter. I was shaking my head at how much more involved it is than I thought it would be. Quite the experience."

Lex decided against bringing up the tar thing. She already knew that he'd insisted on buying new jeans for the girls—not one pair, but three pairs each, in different colors. "I can see how it would be. You haven't spent a lot of time around your nieces in the past couple years, have you?" She realized how critical that sounded, which surprisingly hadn't been her intent. "I meant—"

"No worries," he said as they approached her truck, but his tone had cooled. "I only have them in the mornings."

"What do you do in the afternoons?"

"Rebuild the garage, practice at Hennessey's place." He turned to face her as she dug the keys out of her pocket. "You should come see me practice sometime."

Her gaze jerked up, and then she laughed. "I'm not one of your buckle bunnies."

"Didn't say you were." But the way that his eyes drifted down to her lips made unexpected heat unfurl inside of her. *What the heck?*

She cocked her head and asked coolly, "Then why would you want me to watch you practice?"

"Since my sister works for you, it seemed like a way to make peace."

"Me watching you?"

He smiled a little, the cockiness back. "Hey, I didn't think you'd accept if I asked you out for a drink, so this seemed like the next best thing. You can watch me get smeared into the dirt."

Lex smiled in spite of herself.

"I thought you'd like that," Grady said with an easy grin, and once again she felt the prickles of awareness, the pooling of heat in her midsection. Crazy.

And he knew she was reacting to him. She could see it in the way he was smiling at her.

"How about we agree to make peace?" she asked, wondering if she moved closer if he might try to kiss her. The signals were there, and she couldn't help speculating as to his motivation. She had to believe it was a power thing—payback for meddling in his life— and that was exactly why he wouldn't be kissing her tonight.

"Have it your way," he said with a smile. He patted the hood of her truck. "But if you ever reconsider that smeared-in-the-dirt thing, I'm there every afternoon from five to seven."

Chapter Four

It was exactly five thirty when Lex parked at the end of a line of trucks at Hennessey's, but she didn't get out of her rig immediately. A few guys had glanced her way as she drove by, but now they were once again focused on the small arena. The arena she was in no hurry to see.

She figured she'd give the boys some time to warm up. Yes. Maybe she'd purposely miss watching Grady's ride. The important thing was that she was there, showing him that she wasn't afraid to take him up on what had essentially been a dare.

A dare that was costing her.

Did he know that? Was that why he'd asked her here? Because he knew it would be a very, very difficult thing for her to show up at bull-riding practice?

She hadn't been anywhere near a rodeo or practice arena since her dad died. The heart attack could have happened anywhere, but it had happened in the middle of an arena and the sight of her dad collapsing in the dirt a few yards away from the cowboy he'd just saved was burned into her brain. After losing him, she'd had no reason to go to rodeos. No desire to go. In fact, she didn't even like hearing about them, which was difficult, since many of her friends were competitors.

Maybe it *was* time to see what she was capable of. Two years had passed. She'd grieved... Yes, she could do this.

Maybe.

Darn it, she was sweating. And her hands felt as if they might be on the verge of shaking.

Taking a deep breath, she pushed open the door and stepped out, gathered her strength, walked toward the arena. The first thing that struck her was the well-remembered scent of sweaty animals, manure and dirt. The gate opened on the far side of the arena as she approached, and she heard the familiar sounds of heavy hooves hitting dirt, the grunts of the bull as he did his best to dislodge the predator on his back. Lex stopped. For a moment it was too much. She, who never ran, almost turned and walked straight back to her truck.

"Alexa! Lex!"

One of the Hayward twins—Jess, maybe?—hailed her from where he stood leaning on the fence. Her heart squeezed a little at the sight of him. Her dad had coached Jess and Ty when they first started riding in high school, and she'd often come along with him to Hennessey's to watch.

"Hey..." Lex waited until she got a little closer and saw the small scar on his chin to say "...Ty." She leaned on the fence next to him, watched as a red-haired guy she didn't know picked himself up out of the dirt. The bull, who knew his job, was already on his way out the gate. She took one more deep breath, told herself to relax. *Now.*

"Are you here to give pointers?" Ty asked.

"I guess I am," she lied as she caught sight of Grady at the chute. No way was she confessing she was there because of him. He looked up, caught her staring at him and touched his beat-up straw hat with two fingers. Lex's mouth automatically tightened at the cocky gesture, but she worked it into a wry smirk of acknowledgment.

"I guess Grady's doing the Mr. Mom thing," Ty said.

"I'm sure he's good at it," Lex replied absently. He had the mentality of a kid, so he probably got along great with Annie's twins.

"Not from what I hear." Ty craned his neck as Grady's bull half-reared in the chute.

"Rank one," Lex said, settling her forearms on the sun-warmed rail. Her heart was beating faster, but she could do this. So what if she felt like puking?

"Hennessey got some new bulls in a couple days ago. This is one of them."

Grady was talking to some kids who were hanging close to him, no doubt explaining something he was hoping to demonstrate. He gestured at the bull a couple of times, then climbed on. He took the rope, carefully closed his glove around it and pounded his fist so that the rosin beat into the leather.

Lex's heart seemed to creep up into her throat as she watched the familiar routine. That damned glove had better come free. The rope had better not twist around it, hanging him up—

The glove came free.

Within seconds of Grady giving the signal and the gate swinging open, he was sitting in the dirt. Lex pressed the back of her hand against her mouth to keep the laughter that had bubbled up from escaping. It was pure relief, nothing to do with Grady getting smeared in the dirt, as he'd predicted. She'd just watched her first bull ride after her father's heart attack and survived. Her heart was still beating too hard, and her stomach was still tight but she'd make it without puking or turning away. And now her nemesis was picking himself up and beating his hat on his leg to shake off the dust.

"Huh," Ty said from beside her.

"Happens to the best of them," Lex said, glad that the urge to laugh was, for the most part, gone. Grady's balance had been off the instant the bull reared out of the chute, something that probably didn't happen to him often. It was a fluke that it'd happened while she was there. No—more than a fluke. It was a gift. She hadn't had to watch too much of a buck, and now she could leave, pride fully intact.

Grady walked back to where the high school kids were waiting and spent several minutes talking to them. The kids listened earnestly as the next bull was loaded in the chute, then laughed as Grady made a broad gesture and nodded at the next guy up. As the bull rider climbed over the rails, Grady started walking toward Lex and Ty. Lex pushed off the fence and met him halfway.

"Well, you made good on your promise."

"Man of my word," Grady said. Lex wanted to argue with that but realized she couldn't. He'd always been straight with Danielle.

"You know," Lex said as she started walking in the general direction of her truck, taking slow, deliberate steps so it wouldn't appear as if she were in a hurry. "I could give you some pointers."

Pure bull, because there was no way she was hanging around. She'd survived one ride but had no desire to push matters. All she wanted to do, now that she'd proven her point, was to get in her truck and drive away.

"I know what happened."

She smiled at him, noting that his gaze held on her lips a little too long. "And that was?"

"I screwed up."

She laughed in spite of herself. "You did."

He gestured to her truck. "You're pulling out already?"

She turned and leaned back against the warm metal of the bed. "I've seen what I came for."

"And that's all you wanted to see?" Again his gaze dropped to her lips, and Lex started to get the very strong feeling that she was being hit on. By Grady.

It had to be a power play. There was no other explanation. He was trying to unnerve her. When she met his eyes, he smiled at her, his cheeks creasing in a way that no doubt made the buckle bunnies swoon. Even *she* felt like swooning a little. Grady had charisma. In spades. And right now she felt herself responding to that charisma, which would put him firmly in the driver's seat as they dealt with each other.

Wasn't going to happen.

Lex took her keys out of her pocket, jingled them in her hand as she debated. Then she raised her gaze, deliberately locking it with his. When the questioning frown started to draw his eyebrows together, she stepped closer and slid her free hand around the back of his neck, pushing her fingers into his hair in a smooth caress, smiling a little as she did so. He stilled and she could read the *what the?* in his expression. She loved it.

His skin was warm beneath her wrist. A little damp from the late-afternoon sun, a little dusty from the arena. She registered the sensations in a fraction of a second—registered, too, that she liked those things. Then she pulled his head down and kissed him.

Grady's eyes widened as their lips met. Even though her movements had been slow and careful, she'd taken him by surprise and she made it a point to end the kiss before he got his equilibrium back. Which was no easy trick, because once she'd had a taste of him, incredibly, she wanted more. It was all she could do to paste a careless smile on her face as she took a step back. Her heart was beating almost as hard as it had been during his ride.

"What was that?" he asked gruffly.

"That was me winning this round." She moved past him to pull open her truck door, realizing only then that she'd been gripping the keys so tightly that there was an indent in her palm.

"What?"

"Give the matter some thought, Grady. I'm sure you'll figure it out." She climbed into the cab and then said, "On second thought, I'll spell it out. You're challenging me for some reason, and I'm meeting your challenge." She tilted her head, her hair spilling over her shoulder. "Or have I misread things?"

Her only answer was his narrowed gaze, meaning she had it right.

"Later, Grady." She pulled the door shut.

Thankfully he couldn't see that her hands were shaking as she turned the key in the ignition. She'd definitely won that round, but now as she pulled out of the gravel lot next to the practice arena and glanced in the rearview mirror to see Grady standing right where she'd left him, staring after her, she wondered at what cost.

Without thinking she raised her hand and pressed the back against her lips.

She'd kissed Grady Owen.

AFTER LEX'S BIG Ford truck pulled out of the lot, spraying a little gravel on the way, Grady tugged his hat down a notch and turned back to the arena. Ty Hayward quickly shifted his attention to the action in the chutes rather than the action that had just occurred in the parking lot.

What had just happened?

Grady had to admit that he wasn't quite clear, except that Lex had picked up on the fact that he'd been messing with her; that when he asked her to come watch him practice, he hadn't expected her to say yes. In other words, he'd been tossing out challenges gauged to make her feel uncomfortable. And she'd answered. With the big guns.

So what now?

Walk away and forget that kiss?

As if. He'd idly wondered now and again, as guys tended to do, what Lex's sexy mouth would feel like beneath his. He'd never had the slightest intention of finding out, but now he knew. It felt like something he wouldn't mind experiencing again. Kissing Lex had been like tossing back a shot of good whiskey. Gone too soon, yet the aftereffects hung with him.

He smiled grimly as he headed back to the chutes, ignoring the looks the other riders sent his way. He wasn't one to walk away, and he wasn't all that keen on letting Lex drive into the setting sun feeling like a winner. The next time they met up…well, one thing was for certain. Lex wouldn't be taking him by surprise.

Next time he'd walk away the winner.

GRADY HAD A rough time on the garage the next day, smacking his fingers more than once with the hammer, and he felt like blaming Lex each time. The woman had ruined his focus, just as she'd intended. He couldn't stop thinking about the feel of her mouth. That wasn't the way he wanted to think about Lex. It put him off his game.

"What's up with you and Lex?" Annie asked later that afternoon as she pulled cans out of a shopping bag and started storing them on shelves.

Grady had expected word to get around. A guy simply didn't kiss someone in a parking lot in front of a lot of gossipy cowboys without instigating rumor and innuendo.

"Nothing."

She shot him a glance from under her arm as she set a can on the shelf above her. "You two didn't kiss in the parking lot at Hennessey's?"

"Well, yeah. We did that. But there's nothing to it."

"You and Lex just kissed."

He shrugged, hating that he was having this conversation.

"All right." She reached for another soup can.

"Kristen found a salamander today," he said, grasping at whatever he could to distract his sister.

"She didn't let it go in the house, did she?"

This mother radar was amazing stuff. "Just for a while."

Annie gave a casual nod and folded the paper bag, putting it in the official paper-bag place next to the refrigerator. "And that salamander is now…?"

"Back at the creek." Even though the girls had pleaded for Grady to make a habitat out of a shoe box, he'd managed to convince them that the salamander had a wife and kids and they would be very lonely without him.

"Good."

Katie wandered into the kitchen then, her lips still stained red from the Popsicle she'd had earlier that day. "We caught a lizard today."

"Salamander," Grady automatically corrected.

"He's back with his wife now."

"As all good salamanders should be," Annie agreed, reaching out to stroke her daughter's hair. "Since when do you eat the red Popsicles?"

"The blue ones are all melted."

Annie shot a look at Grady. "Long story," he said.

"Where is your sister?"

"Making her boots shiny for tomorrow."

Tomorrow was the first day of riding lessons. The girls had been talking about it all day long. Annie had bought them new boots but, according to Katie, had drawn the line at Western shirts. "We can't 'ford them," Katie had whispered conspiratorially.

Another small twist of the guilt knife. Grady should have spent more time in Montana during the off-season, even if the training opportunities were limited. His nieces needed spoiling, and he was going to take care of the Western shirt issue tomorrow after lessons.

Annie opened the fridge and took out the stew she'd made the day before. "I know the lessons take away from building time—"

"I don't mind." Watching the twins took away from building time. It seemed he'd barely get started and there'd be a cry of "Uncle Grady!" followed by a minor emergency—a shoe stuck tight in a pant leg, a salamander under the sofa. That kind of stuff. And the reading took time. Just before Grady took the girls to Emily the sitter's house, for the afternoons, the three of them settled on the sofa and the girls took turns reading aloud. They were hell-bent on winning library summer reading awards because one of the prizes was an ice cream free-for-all.

After setting the stew on the counter, Annie turned to him, brushing aside a hank of hair. "I'm not going to lie—having you here is a godsend. Not that you can't go back when it's time," she added hurriedly. "It's just nice to have some backup for a while." She turned to put the stew on the stove. "Once school starts, I won't have to worry about morning day care. Emily will pick them up after school and keep them until I'm off work." She gave her head a shake. "Second grade already. How did that happen?"

"Time flies," Grady agreed. Pretty soon he'd be too old to ride bulls and would have to look at a second career, and he was seriously considering something in the building trades. But he still had a few good years in him, and he needed to keep at the top of his game as much as possible, training when he had a free moment and spending more time at Hennessey's.

LEX DIDN'T MAKE it into the store on Thursday because of a dental appointment, and when she walked in the door early Friday morning, Danielle gave her the eye—the concerned friend eye—as she finished hanging a red gingham apron next to a display of red-and-white cooking implements.

"What?" Lex asked. She wandered closer and picked an apron out of the cardboard box sitting on the floor next to her friend. They were handmade, probably by one of her grandmothers, since Danielle concentrated solely on quilting. When Danielle didn't answer the question, she looked up again.

"Did you really kiss Grady?" Danielle asked in a voice pitched a little higher than usual.

"It was to make a point," Lex said with an overly casual shrug before she handed over the apron she held and reached for the last apron in the box.

Danielle frowned at her. "And that point would be...?"

"The point was that he can't mess with me."

"How was he messing with you?"

"He was kind of hitting on me." She set the apron on the table next to her, ignoring the fact that it didn't belong in a display of Western wine racks. If she held on to it any longer, she might wrinkle it with a death grip.

Danielle's eyebrows arched. "Grady?" She plucked the apron off the table and draped it near a setting of Western table service.

"It wasn't for real. He was—" Lex made an impatient gesture "—he walked me to my car after we ran into each other at Shardlow's. Then he asked me to come and watch him practice, because he knew I wouldn't, so of course I had to." She paused, realizing it didn't sound like all that much. "You had to be there," she finished.

"Sounds like it." Danielle nodded thoughtfully. "How about I stay out of this?"

"There's nothing to stay out of."

"If you say so."

Annie came in through the back door then, calling a hello as she hung her tote bag on the hooks near the door. She turned toward Lex and Danielle and smiled awkwardly. Lex had never in her life seen Annie do anything awkwardly. The woman was warmth incarnate, unless someone riled her. The only explanation was that Annie knew about the kiss, so Lex saw no other option than to take the offensive—for the good of the store, of course.

"Yes, I kissed your brother, but only to make a point." There. Out in the open.

"I heard," Annie said matter-of-factly. "Good luck with that point thing."

There was a heavy silence, and then Danielle giggled from behind them. Both Lex and Annie turned to look at her; then a second later Annie laughed, too. Lex let out a breath and felt her lips begin to curve.

"That's out of the way," Danielle said as she reached for the smock she wore while tidying up the store, "and if yesterday was anything to judge by, we have a full day ahead of us, so let's get at it."

It was a full day. Tourists were on the road and many wanted to take home fun Western memorabilia, which was what Annie Get Your Gun was all about. By closing time they'd sold enough that Annie had started unpacking boxes from their new shipment ahead of time and Lex had made a long list of jewelry pieces she needed to replace.

"Grandma is going to be so thrilled about the aprons. I bet I'll have to drive her to the fabric store again this weekend." Danielle finished refolding her remaining quilts and arranging them over the brass bedstead they used for display purposes.

"And you sold three quilts," Annie said, sounding impressed. "That would be three, no, make that four, years of work for me."

Danielle laughed. "Not if you take a shortcut."

Annie frowned and Lex explained, "She pieces the quilt tops and then sends them out to be quilted by a professional."

"I used to do all the quilting by hand, but that's not cost-effective unless you're making heirloom pieces."

"I'd still be looking at the three-or-four-year range, even with the shortcut," Annie said on a sigh. "Since the girls were born, I haven't had a lot of time to indulge in any kind of hobby."

"From what I hear, the time comes all too soon," Danielle said.

"You're right. They're in second grade. Can you believe it?"

They'd been five when Danielle broke up with Grady, three when they'd started dating.

"No," Danielle said simply.

After closing, they tidied up the store. Then before heading out the door, Annie said to Lex, "Please, no matter what happens with you and Grady, never feel like you have to be awkward around me. Grady can handle his own life."

"And vice versa," Lex said. "But I think Grady and I are done lobbing volleys at each other." As things stood now, she was the winner and she wanted to keep it that way. Why start another battle she might well not win?

"Yeah," Annie said, slowly, sounding like a sister who knew her brother well enough not to partake in Lex's fantasy. "Maybe."

Danielle simply lifted her eyebrows.

And Lex got the idea that maybe the battle had been won, but the war was not over.

Chapter Five

Saturday morning Lex was up early, grooming the mares she was taking to Jared's riding lessons. Rosie, Daphne and Lacy were all over twenty years old, with quiet temperaments suited to beginners. Daphne had been her father's backup horse when he wasn't riding cranky old Snuff, and Rosie and Lacy had been her 4-H and rodeo horses. All three were now retired from ranch work but were perfect for her cousin Jared's purposes.

She pulled into the fairgrounds a little before 8:00 a.m. The lessons started at 9:00 a.m., but Jared wanted the high school students who would help him for the next six weeks to warm up the horses.

"Lex, thanks for doing this," he said as she got out of the truck. He introduced his crew of four helpers to her, then sent a couple of girls to unload the mares.

She shaded her eyes as she looked at the stands. "I think I'll hang out. Make sure everything goes all right. And if you need an extra pair of hands, I'm here."

He smiled at her. "Always glad to have some backup." He shifted his weight and cocked his head. "So, what's the deal with you and Grady?"

The curse of close relatives who'd helped you

through the roughest time of your life. They tended to ask direct questions instead of wondering what was going on.

"Nothing. Just—" she shrugged as casually as she could "—a long story. Not very interesting." She smiled brightly, and Jared took the hint.

"Yeah. Okay…" He took a look around the fairgrounds. His crew was mounted, and he walked over to open the gate so that they could ride the horses around the small arena where he'd be giving lessons, warming them up before the students arrived.

"I'll be in the stands," Lex called after him. She went to the truck and pulled out her hat and her phone and then climbed the bleacher stairs to a seat high enough to see clearly but low enough that she could help if there were any unforeseen problems.

An unforeseen problem arrived twenty minutes later in the form of one cocky bull rider. Lex practically smacked her forehead as Grady's truck pulled up and two little girls with bouncing pigtails got out. Of course Annie's twins would be taking lessons. And of course Grady would bring them here because Annie was running the store.

Yay.

Grady helped one of the little girls adjust her belt, kneeling and fiddling with the buckle, which was nearly as big as the kid. When he stood, the other twin grabbed his hand and pulled him toward the arena fence. Jared intercepted them, had a brief discussion and then the girls raced back to the truck and came back with helmets.

Lex pulled her hat a little lower over her eyes, as if it would make her invisible. It didn't work. When two more cars showed up and four more kids joined Annie's twins, Grady turned toward the stands. And even at a distance, she could see him smile. It wasn't a friendly smile, either.

Lex shifted in her seat as he said a few words to Jared before making a beeline toward the stands.

He walked up the steps and took a seat a few feet from Lex.

"Morning," he said as he settled, leaning back on his elbows on the seat behind him.

"Yes," Lex agreed. She did her best to ignore him, but it was like trying to ignore a panther sunning himself nearby. His sheer proximity made her edgy, and it irritated her. "There's a whole lot of bleacher here," she finally said.

"Do you want me to move?"

"Maybe I don't want people to keep questioning me about you."

"Whose fault is that?" he asked mildly.

"Mine. But you were asking for it."

"I was asking you to kiss me?"

Lex wasn't about to be put off by an innocence act. "You were trying to provoke me."

"You made first contact."

"If you're not careful, I'll make second contact."

Grady's eyes narrowed thoughtfully, and it was all Lex could do to keep from swallowing drily. But she wasn't going to look at his mouth—even though she wanted to.

This was a habit she needed to break. Especially when it seemed totally possible that Grady was reading her mind. Why else would that mouth have formed an ironic curve when she lost her battle with herself?

"No. You won't."

And there he had her. No. She wouldn't. The element of surprise was gone, as was the shock factor.

"You're right," she said casually. "I don't like to repeat myself."

Grady snorted, then lifted his chin as the high school kids helped the students mount.

"I take it your nieces haven't ridden much?"

"No. Something I'm hoping to rectify. I'm glad Annie signed them up for lessons."

"So *you* didn't sign them up just to come here and annoy me?"

"Didn't even know you'd be here," he said, keeping his eyes on the arena. "Do not overestimate your own importance."

Lex managed not to elbow him and instead followed his gaze. One of his nieces, mounted on one of Jared's horses, was sitting tall and confident, but the other little girl, riding gentle Daphne, was practically curled over the saddle horn.

"She'll probably relax as the lesson progresses," Lex said.

"I hope so." Grady once again leaned back, making a show of being unconcerned, but Lex could feel tension radiating off him. His niece unfurled a bit as the lesson progressed, and Grady leaned forward, watching as the kids slowly rode in circles, then reversed and rode the other way. The high school kids would occasionally bring riders to the side and reposition their feet or hands.

The lesson lasted another thirty minutes, during which time Lex and Grady maintained a mutual silence. He was too focused on his nieces to banter with her, and she was too busy wondering how it was that she was sharing an empty grandstand with Grady Owen.

Life was strange sometimes.

After the lesson, Grady's nieces rushed him, and Lex saw that they were both wearing silver championship bull-riding buckles on their pink belts. The kind of buckles the average bull rider coveted.

"Hey, guys. You did great." He pointed behind them. "Looks like there's a meeting. Come on." He took their hands, and they went to where Jared was speaking to the parents and riders.

Lex headed around her trailer and found her mares tied there and a teenager busily unsaddling them. Lex said hello and helped, carrying the lightweight nylon saddles to the equipment trailer hitched to one of the trucks.

Before driving away, Lex took one last look at Grady and his nieces. This was a side of him she hadn't expected. The Grady Owen she knew was totally self-centered. He didn't go all tense because one of his nieces was having a bad day on horseback.

Lex turned onto the road leading out of the fairgrounds, glad to be putting distance between herself and a certain bull rider. She wasn't going to spend the next six Saturday mornings in the grandstands with Grady, but then again, she wasn't going to hide out in her truck, either. So the solution was…

To put the situation out of her mind until next week.

AFTER LEX GOT HOME, she unloaded the horses and gave them a small portion of grain. She gave the goat and donkeys even smaller portions, handed out treats to all the dogs, then put everyone back into their respective yards, kennels, corrals and pens so that she could drive back to town and get the supplies for the new jewelry designs knocking around in her head.

"You'll be out before you know it," she told Dave the Terror when the little terrier protested being shut up in the yard so soon after being released. All she had to do was to hit the grocery store and the hardware store and then check in with Danielle at Annie Get Your Gun before heading home again. All in all, not too bad as far as errand day went. Or so she thought until she spotted a familiar truck parked in front of the hardware store after pulling into the lot. Todd Lundgren. She'd rather cozy up to Grady in the bleachers for a couple of weeks than come within fifty feet of Todd even once.

For a brief moment, she considered swinging the truck in an arc and coming back later.

Except that she was no coward.

During high school, she and Todd hadn't paid much attention to each other. He'd been busy commanding the social scene and captaining teams, while Lex had been more of a get-the-job-done-and-graduate person. Their paths rarely crossed, but when Todd returned to town to take over the family business six months ago, he suddenly seemed to realize that Lex existed. And apparently she was supposed to be pleased about that.

He'd zeroed his sights in on her one night at Shardlow's Bar, bought her a drink, which she accepted out of politeness, and then, after some amount of flirting and casual boasting, had asked her to leave with him. Lex politely declined his offer. She'd been amazed he'd even made it on such a short acquaintanceship.

Todd had seemed mildly stunned at her refusal.

Apparently thinking she was playing hard to get—
because he was well-off financially, had played one
year of pro baseball and was good-looking to boot—
he gave her another chance. This time Lex was quite
clear about the possibility of them going out—wasn't
going to happen. She did it quietly, which she thought
was rather decent of her. Quiet or not, Todd hadn't
taken it well. So it went with spoiled golden boys. He
wanted what he couldn't have.

Well, he needed to get it through his thick skull that
he wasn't getting her.

When she walked through the automatic doors,
Todd was standing near the checkout counter—tall
and blond, with the perfect amount of scruff on his
face—talking to one of the guys who'd been at Shardlow's the night she shut him down. So much for getting
in and out of the store without seeing him. He smirked
at her as she went by, and he was still at the counter
when she came back with solder, wire and some copper sheeting. She wondered if it was her imagination,
or if he was posing.

"Home repairs?" he asked.

"Something like that." She dug through her purse
for her bank card and paid for the items.

"Need help getting this stuff to the car?"

"Thank you, no." *Do not engage. Do* not *engage.*

Todd touched a finger to his ball cap, pushed off
the counter and left the associate to load her purchases
in a bag.

Lex gave a mental sigh of relief only to find him
waiting for her just outside the door.

"I have this theory," he said.

"Let me take a wild guess." Lex palmed her keys,

in case she had to deck him. "You think I secretly like you."

"I don't think you're immune. I just moved too fast. You're not used to that."

She smiled humorlessly. Refrained from saying, *Dream on.* He wasn't stupid or delusional. He was offended about being shut down, and to him, the ultimate victory would be for her to admit she'd made a ridiculous mistake.

That was her best guess, anyway.

"Have a good one, Todd." She unlocked her door and got into her truck, and then, in an uncharacteristic but not altogether unwarranted move, locked it again. She wasn't afraid of Todd Lundgren, but she didn't want him climbing into her truck, either.

The one saving grace was that Todd's newly inherited ranch was closer to Dillon than Gavin, so he spent more time there. She only ran into him every now and again, and if she saw him in a bar, she left.

"Everything okay?" Danielle looked up from the catalogue she was perusing as Lex walked in through the back door. That was when Lex realized that she was frowning.

"Everything is fine, except that I ran into Todd at the hardware store. He's still at it."

"I swear," Danielle said as she closed the book. "You're his great white whale. He's not going to rest until he—"

Lex gave her a look. "Did you just call me a whale?"

"Symbolically."

"Thank you for that small favor," she said primly.

"Bad analogy."

"Let's move on from Todd," Lex said. "I have some ideas for some copper jewelry, which would be a lot more cost-effective than sterling. I'm going to work up some sample pieces today and tomorrow."

"Great idea! We can set up another display area near the pottery. Kelly's behind on her schedule because of her new job, and that'd be a great way to fill that space."

"Hey," Annie said as she joined them in the back room. "I thought I heard you. How were lessons?"

Lessons. Right. Todd had blasted that stuff right out of her head. "The girls did great." Lex would leave it to Grady to explain that one of the girls did better than the other. That didn't seem to be her place. "They rode for half an hour, and Grady was watching them like a mother hen."

"I'm so glad it worked out. If he wasn't here, I don't think they could have made it."

"He's a good uncle," Lex agreed, rather proud of herself for being able to say something nice about the guy to his sister—and something true at that.

The bell rang in the other room, and Annie ducked out of the room to greet the customers.

"Hiring her was a good call," Lex said.

"Yep," Danielle agreed. "Sometimes you've got to move beyond the past for the good of everyone."

Unless that past involved Grady or Todd Lundgren. There were limits to moving on.

GRADY KNEW SOMETHING was up when Kristen polished her cowboy boots on Friday afternoon and Katie didn't. Katie also mentioned about six times that her stomach hurt. Bad.

"Do you want to miss riding lessons?"

"Maybe this once," Katie replied in a voice so low he could barely hear her.

"But you want to go back next week."

"Maybe."

And maybe he had a problem on his hands. "You want to talk?"

"No."

"All right." He had two choices. He could either let things be or see if Kristen had some information he could cajole her into sharing.

Kristen did not need to be cajoled. "Katie's afraid."

"Of what?"

"Falling. She wants to sit with you and the lady tomorrow instead of riding."

Grady blew out a breath. He hadn't planned on sitting with the lady, even though he seemed to be doing a lot of thinking about her. She made it clear the other night that, kiss or no kiss, she pretty much despised him.

The next day as he drove the girls to lessons, Grady debated how best to handle the matter. Katie was not a happy camper, and he needed to do something about it.

When a bull rider got to the point that he was afraid to get on a bull, it was time to find another career. You could tell a guy how to improve his technique, how to center and relax before his ride, but there was no talking him into trying to overcome his fear, because the consequences were dire. Therefore Grady had no experience in calming fears. The only fears he'd had to calm were those of people afraid of something happening to him. And then he simply said, "Don't worry. I've got this."

He parked the truck, and the girls got out. Kristen looked as if she wanted to head over to where her horse was being groomed, but she held back.

Grady bent close to Katie and pointed to where Lex was unloading her mares. "Do you want to go over to see your horse?"

Katie pressed her lips together and didn't answer. Kristen said to Grady, "We'll go say hello to the horse and the lady and then we can go see my horse."

"All right," Katie said. Kristen took her hand and they walked over to Lex, Grady following a few paces behind. When they got to the trailer, Lex glanced over her shoulder at the girls, then smiled. A breathtaking smile. Grady almost stopped in his tracks. *Wow.*

Had he ever seen Lex look like that before?

"Hi, guys. Ready to ride?"

"Kind of," Katie said.

"Kind of?" Lex lowered the brush she'd been using to sweep the road dust off the mare's back and cocked her head at Katie, who nodded that yes, she was kind of ready to ride.

"We're working through a few things. I need to speak to Jared." Grady met Lex's puzzled gaze. "Would you mind if the girls hung here with you for a few minutes?" He gave her a look that promised an explanation later, and she gave a small nod.

"Not at all." She turned back to her brushing. "You might want to stand back, or you'll end up wearing the dirt I'm brushing off these guys."

The girls obediently stepped back and Grady went to find Jared, who was discussing the day's lesson with his helpers. Grady explained the situation, and Jared told him that he'd talk to Katie, but if she was truly afraid then he wasn't about to force her onto a horse. Grady was in full agreement, but after the talk with Jared, Katie told Grady she'd try again, because Jared said she could stop whenever she wanted. She lasted for half of the lesson, until it was time to trot; then she raised her hand and asked if she could be done.

Grady met her at the gate, where he'd stayed with a small group of parents instead of sitting in the stands with Lex, and helped her dismount.

"That was good," he said.

Katie nodded and he could tell that she was embarrassed at having quit early, but her instinct for survival was stronger than her fear of embarrassment.

It was a quiet ride home. Kristen had enjoyed the lesson, but she wasn't about to talk about it when Katie so obviously didn't enjoy herself.

"Give her time," Annie said later that evening when she and Grady were sitting on the porch. "Katie has always been more cautious than Kristen."

"Neither of them struck me as cautious until riding lessons."

"Katie's a little nervous around big animals," Annie said. "She takes after me. Kristen takes after you."

"In some ways that's more worrisome than Katie being afraid of falling off a horse."

"I'm not touching that one," Annie replied, sending him an amused look.

She didn't seem that concerned, so Grady decided that maybe he didn't need to be concerned. "How's work?"

"I love it." She leaned her head back, a smile still

playing on her lips. "I can't believe that something went right in my life for a change."

"Hey, you have a free sitter."

"Well, there is that," she said. "It took a tornado to get me my free sitter, but—" she gave her head a small shake "—whatever it takes." Her expression sobered. "I really appreciate you coming back to help."

"I should have been back earlier. As in years ago."

"Why do you say that?"

"It was selfish of me to winter in Oklahoma when I could have been here."

She gave him a hard look, similar to the one she'd given him after seeing the aftermath of the twins' cake-making efforts. "You're my brother, Grady. With a life of your own. You owe me nothing."

"I disagree." They sat in silence, and then he said, "Do you see much of Lex at the store? And don't read anything into the question."

"She comes by a couple times a week. We have business meetings on Wednesdays, and she helps cover when Danielle is busy with her wedding preparations." She gave him a sidelong look. "And just so I don't read anything into it, why do you ask?"

"She owns the horse Katie rides. Maybe if Katie had some one-on-one, it would help."

Annie gave a considering nod. "It might." She leaned forward, her hands on her knees. "I'm not sure how I feel about asking Lex for special favors after they did me the favor of hiring me."

"It'll be a favor to me, and I have no problem asking."

"Do you think she'll do a favor for you? When you

were dating Danielle, I think it's safe to say that she hated you."

"She thought I was going to hurt Danielle. She told me that to my face. A couple of times."

"You did hurt Danielle."

"And let me tell you, that hasn't helped things between me and Lex."

"You kissed her."

"She kissed me. It was short." *Too short.* "Like a peck."

"That's not what I heard." He frowned at his sister, and she added, "Not one version of the story involved a peck."

"How many versions did you hear?" he asked wearily.

"At least three. You know that cowboys gossip like old ladies."

"Unfortunately."

She looked back up at the stars. "I don't have a clue as to what's going on between you two."

"Don't try," Grady advised. "And as to favors, I'd be doing the tutoring, but I want to use the horse Katie rides in class, and that's where Lex comes in."

"I do not want my daughter in the middle of cross fire between you two."

"No cross fire." He glanced down at his hands, clasped loosely between his knees. "I think it's important to see if we can address this fear of Katie's, but you're her mom."

"I don't want her to grow up nervous about horses. She's already afraid of big dogs."

"So I can ask Lex?"

She studied him as she used to when he was trying to put one over on her when they were kids. Finally she said, "If you think it will help."

Chapter Six

"You have to go already?" Danielle's great-grandmother asked as Lex gathered her purse and jacket. They'd had quite the summit today, during which the proper shade of pink was agreed upon.

"Vet appointment," Lex said, hating to leave Danielle with no backup as the Perry women went over catalogs and fabric samples from various bridal houses. There was definitely a wide range of tastes in the Perry family, and poor Danielle spent as much time protecting feelings as she did trying to choose proper dresses. Originally she'd wanted the bridesmaids to choose their own dresses in any shade of pink they wanted. Her grandmother about fell over, having come from the everything-matching era, and after Great-granny had shown up at the store with the paint chips, they compromised on allowing the five bridesmaids to choose their own styles of dress in the exact same color. Then the fight was on for length. Mom wanted formal length. Danielle wanted tea length. Great-granny, surprisingly, agreed with Danielle, and Grandma was undecided. Lex knew she'd never wear her dress again, so she was all for whatever made Danielle happy and cast her vote for tea length before announcing that she had to go.

"Nothing serious, I hope." Danielle's mother looked up from where she was laying out ever more samples.

"Just routine teeth floating. I scheduled before I knew we were meeting," Lex said.

"You've cleared your calendar for the Bozeman trip, right?" All three older Perry women waited for Lex to answer Great-granny's question.

Lex smiled. "I wouldn't miss it." Who wouldn't want to travel with three opinionated women to visit several bridal boutiques?

"I'll see you at work," Danielle said as she walked Lex to the door.

"Good luck," Lex murmured. "Wish I could stay."

"No, you don't," Danielle replied wryly. "But I know you would have." She glanced over her shoulder at the kitchen table, just visible through the arched doorway, then let her head fall forward in a comical gesture of defeat. "I love them, but...elopement sounds so inviting right now."

"Elopement would kill them."

"I know. So I forge on." She smiled. "Enjoy your vet appointment... Kind of wish I could go with you."

Lex got home and had barely changed into her old jeans before the veterinary utility truck pulled up next to the barn and a tall guy with dark blond hair got out. Dr. Caldwell, her regular horse vet, was easing into retirement, and she'd yet to meet the new vet who was buying into the practice.

After quickly pulling her hair into a ponytail, Lex headed out the door, crossing the driveway to where the vet was unpacking his tools from a side utility panel. He straightened as she approached and flashed her a smile. "Good to see you again," he said.

Lex frowned as she searched her memory for good-looking, blond vets and came up empty. "You don't remember me, do you?" he asked after shutting the truck door. Lex shook her head. Surely she would remember a guy like this. He was tall, muscular and had excellent bones.

"Pete Randall."

Lex's eyebrows shot up. "Petey?" The kid who'd spent summers with his grandparents a few miles down the road. He'd been awkward, skinny and had never seemed at home in a rural setting. They'd met at various community functions, but he'd always stayed close to his grandparents and if she recalled, he used to be reading a lot.

"One and the same," he said with an easy grin. "Although I'd like to forget the Petey handle."

Lex laughed. "All right. Peter."

"Just plain Pete. I bought into Dr. Caldwell's practice."

"I'd heard about that, but I had no idea it was you, or that you'd become a vet." Lex frowned a little as she came to his side of the truck. "Weren't you afraid of horses?" She vaguely recalled a 4-H event where he'd tried to avoid them.

"Yeah. It kind of held me back early on in my studies," he admitted with a half smile. "But I got over it. So, where are my patients?"

Lex took him to the corral where the mares and Snuff stood sunning themselves. "Give me a minute to catch them and we can get started." She disappeared into the tack room to get the halters. "I was at a wedding-planning summit and got back later than expected."

"Anyone I might remember?"

"Danielle Perry."

"I remember. All the boys had a crush on her."

"Did you?"

"I was afraid of girls," he said. "I got over that, too."

That was a win for the female population. Little Petey had grown into one heck of a man.

In short order Lex had the three older mares and the cranky gelding caught and tied to the hitching rail. Peter went to work smoothing their teeth so that they could eat effectively, and Lex watched, impressed with his technique.

"They're all in pretty good shape," he said when he was finished and had put his files away. "And I see by their records that you keep them on a regular schedule." Horses tended to need more dental care as they aged, and Lex stayed on top of it.

"I'm a vet's dream," she said. Peter leaned against the hood of his truck and swept his gaze over the pens where the donkeys were eating their morning rations. The dogs were pressing their noses against the front yard fence, and Felicity was sunning herself on a fence post nearby while the goat ate weeds at the base of the post. Out in the field her three young horses grazed.

"Is this the entire crew?" he asked.

"I have four cows that I run with the neighbor," she said, pointing at the fields adjoining her small property. The cows were coming in to water at the stock pond with their calves by their sides. There was a bit of an awkward pause; then Peter glanced down at his watch.

"I need to get moving if I'm going to make my next call on time." He pushed off the hood and held out a hand. "Good to see you, Alexa. I'm sure we'll meet again."

"And again and again," she agreed with a smile. She took good care of her animals.

As soon as Pete was in his truck, she started cleaning the goat pen, then stopped when another truck pulled into her driveway.

Grady.

This was an interesting turn of events, Grady coming to her turf. She crossed the pen to the gate as he parked next to the barn, thinking that he'd better have a good reason for being there.

He got out of his truck and came around the front, and Lex couldn't help noticing that while he wasn't as tall as Pete, he somehow had more presence. And that she responded to that presence.

"I need to shut off a faucet," she said before he said hello or whatever it was he'd come to say. Water was pouring over the side of the donkey tank, so she brushed past him on her way to the pen. Grady followed, his boots crunching on the gravel behind her, making her wonder why she hadn't noticed the sound of Pete's boots when they traveled almost the same route.

Because she wasn't so freaking aware of Pete.

"You have a lot of animals," Grady said once the faucet was off and she'd turned back to him.

"I like animals," Lex said drily as the goat wandered up behind Grady and sniffed curiously at his pant leg.

He tipped back his hat so she could get a good look

at his gray eyes. And the scar along his dark hairline. "I have a favor to ask of you."

"Yeah?" Her eyes narrowed. What kind of favor could he possibly ask of her? And why was her heart beating faster?

"Would you consider giving my niece Katie, the one that's having a hard time in lessons, some one-on-one time in the evenings?"

Not at all what she expected…but then she'd had no idea what to expect. "Why me and not Jared?"

"I think if Katie spent time with the horse she rides—which happens to be your horse—in a more private environment, she might get over her fear of falling."

Great. A legitimate reason. Lex dropped her chin and studied the ground between her boots as she debated over options and realized she only had two. Saying yes and helping a kid, or saying no because the kid's uncle set her on edge.

"Well?" he said after a few long seconds, and she had to give him credit for sounding less than confident.

Lex's mouth tightened as she brought her gaze up to his, saw that there was no hint of challenge in his expression. Only a question. Would she help his niece? "How can I say no to something like that?"

"Because I'm involved?"

"I have to say that it doesn't exactly sweeten the deal."

He laughed, and something inside her did a bit of a free fall. Which in turn irritated her. She was not going to be one of the many sucked in by Grady Owen's charm and good looks. She started back to where she'd left the manure fork, Grady walking a few feet away from her, even though it felt closer.

He's just a guy.

A guy there about his niece. This had nothing to do with Danielle or old vendettas or getting back at her for kissing him in the parking lot at Hennessey's in front of his rodeo buddies. She stopped near his truck, hoping that once she gave her answer, he wouldn't prolong the visit. "Fine. When do you want to stop by?"

The goat chose that moment to rub the side of her head on the back of Grady's thighs, knocking him a few steps forward. Lex automatically moved back, keeping a good distance between them. "Tomorrow evening after Annie gets home?"

"I'll be covering for Danielle at the store all this week." Her friend was escaping to Wyoming with her fiancé for a much-needed break from wedding planning.

"Oh." A shadow crossed Grady's face.

"But I don't mind doing this," she said gruffly. "For the kid." And only for the kid. "How about six o'clock?"

"Six it is." He reached down to rub the goat's bony head. "See you then." The words were barely out of his mouth before he was moving toward the driver's side of the truck, apparently making good his escape before she could change her mind.

Lex wrapped her arms around herself as he opened the door, then realized how blatantly self-protective her body language was and dropped her arms back to her sides. She had no need to protect herself from Grady Owen, of all people. She could hold her own with him just fine, thank you very much.

But there was something in the way he smiled as he waved at her before putting the truck in gear that made her wonder if he wasn't reading her thoughts and plotting another move to upset her equilibrium *after* she helped him with his niece.

Well, plot away, Mr. Owen. You are not getting the better of me.

KRISTEN WAS NOT happy about her twin going to Lex's farm without her, even after Grady had explained how it would help her if she got to meet the horses by herself.

"But you'll be there."

"Yes."

"And the lady."

"Yes, the lady will be there." He had to fight to keep from smiling at Lex being called "the lady." When he thought of ladies, he thought of women dressed up for afternoon tea or something, and that image didn't fit Lex one bit. But it did get him thinking about what she might look like dressed up, and he came to the tentative conclusion that she probably looked best as he knew her—dressed in denim, with a button-front shirt and boots, silver earrings flashing through her loose dark hair. Lex definitely rocked that look, better even than Danielle, because Lex had that aura of toughness about her that perfectly complemented denim and boots, yet there was a whisper of vulnerability there, too, which made a guy wonder if she was wearing lace under her clothes.

"I want to go, too." Kristen yanked him back to the present.

"How about we let Katie go alone this first time?

You help your mom like we planned, and we'll talk when we get back."

After winning the battle with Kristen, he had to deal with Katie, who was certain she didn't want to go without Kristen.

"I think it'll be a mistake to take them together." Annie said when he had discussed the matter with her over a beer on the porch after she'd returned home from work. "Kristen doesn't want to miss out on any horse stuff, and Katie will happily let her take over. Do you want me to be the bad guy?"

"I'll do it." Parenthood, Grady was rapidly discovering, was challenging on many levels, yet he found he rather enjoyed the challenge. The tears, not so much, but he made his way through the waterworks by sticking to his guns, and eventually Kristen and Katie accepted the fact that only one of them was going to Lex's farm the first time. After that, they'd talk again. He only hoped the talk wouldn't involve tears all over again. Kid tears melted his heart, but it wasn't going to do anyone any good if he caved when one of the girls cried.

"Kristen has got to promise not to get ahead of me in reading," Katie said. They were getting close to the qualification mark for the library dedicated reader awards. They could practically taste the ice cream, and Katie was shopping for a new swimming suit online for the pool party that followed.

"We'll read together when we get back," Grady promised her. "I think we can finish that dog book tonight."

The next evening after Annie got home from work, Katie and Grady set out for Lex's farm. Katie was not her usual chattering self, and after a few attempts to cajole her out of her mood, Grady let her be. Sometimes it was best to address fears quietly, as he'd learned during his years of bull riding. Katie was dealing with issues, and he would allow her to do it in her own way.

Lex met the truck as he parked next to the barn, smiling at Katie through the open window. "Hi. I hear you've come to visit Daphne."

Katie nodded glumly.

"Good. You can help me clean her up."

Katie's eyes widened. "I thought I had to ride her."

"Nope. We're going to brush her. Maybe put some braids in her hair."

Lex opened the door, and Katie scrambled out of the truck, nearly dropping out of sight as her boots hit the ground. "Will she get ribbons?" Katie asked.

"I can probably find some."

Lex was dressed, as usual, in worn jeans, scuffed boots, and a dusty blue button-front Western shirt, but now he was wondering what she was wearing underneath. Utility cotton? Satin or lace?

He gave his head a quick shake.

"Are you all right?" Lex asked with a frown.

"Fine." He reached out to take Katie's hand and followed Lex to Daphne's pen. The buckskin mare ambled across the pen toward them, and Katie drew back a little. Grady didn't say a word, nor did Lex.

Katie stood where she was as Daphne hung her head over the fence to be petted. Lex rubbed her ears and stroked her mane until Katie came up of her own accord and held out the back of her hand for Daphne to sniff, as Grady had taught her.

Daphne bumped her nose against the little girl's fist, and she laughed nervously. "She did the horse handshake, just like you said she would."

"Do you want to help me brush her?" Lex asked.

"Maybe I'll watch."

"That's fine. I'll brush. You watch. And if you feel like helping, there's a big bucket of brushes there. Remember to always walk up to a horse from the side. Never from the back."

"'Cause they can't see behind them, and it scares them."

"Exactly. Now I want to get the hay and loose dirt off her first, so I'm going to start with a currycomb..."

Grady found a spot of shade near the barn a few yards away and watched as Lex talked and groomed and Katie edged closer, first going through the grooming tools and asking about each one, then delivering them to Lex as she called for them. Especially fascinating was the hoof cleaning, and Grady knew they'd turned a small corner when Katie used the hoof pick to clean out the hoof while Lex held it. And then came the braiding, with Lex doing the braids and Katie handing her bands and ribbons.

"She's so pretty," Katie said as they finished the mane and started the tail. "Will she have ribbons at lessons?"

"I'm sure I can arrange that," Lex said, catching Grady's eye. He raised an eyebrow in response, and then she shifted her gaze back to the horse. Safer territory.

When the last ribbon was tied, Lex called it a night.

"I really don't gotta ride her?"

"Nope. We'll let her go get a drink of water. Speaking of which, I have Kool-Aid."

"Blue?"

"As a matter of fact…"

At the mention of blue Kool-Aid, Katie nodded happily and started skipping ahead of Lex. Grady fell into step with her. "She isn't on top of the horse yet," Lex replied when he expressed his gratitude for his niece's one-eighty.

"She's more comfortable. When I asked you to do this, I expected to do the coaching. I only wanted to borrow the horse."

"I know."

And that was all she said. Finally Grady said, "The place seems to be quieter today."

"I kept the dogs in the house so they wouldn't bum-rush the kid. And I penned up the rest of the menagerie, thinking it might be easier on Kristen if Katie wasn't here communing with a petting zoo without her."

"Wait for us on the porch," Grady called as Katie opened the front gate and started up the walk. "Why *do* you have a petting zoo?" he asked, slowing his steps.

Lex gave a shrug. "They all needed homes."

"And you needed something to take care of?" Her expression instantly shuttered. Grady stuck a thumb into his front pocket and casually added, "It's nice that you have the resources to rescue these guys. Give them a good home."

She eyed him, her gaze wavering on the edge of suspicion, and then she apparently decided to give him the benefit of the doubt. "Dad left me well off."

"He was a good guy."

Lex merely nodded, hooking a thumb in a belt loop, mirroring his pose. "I'd better get your niece her Kool-Aid. You want something?"

"Kool-Aid is fine."

"It's the blue kind," she said with a straight face. "It'll stain your lips."

"I'll live."

So he and Lex and Katie all had a glass of blue Kool-Aid and sure enough, it stained lips—which was probably why he kept looking at Lex's mouth.

Right.

Shortly after Katie's glass was empty, they headed home to find Kristen waiting with her nose pressed against the screen door.

"How'd it go?" Annie asked after Katie and Kristen holed up in their bedroom to compare notes. Then she frowned at him, cocking her head to see him better. "Blue Kool-Aid?"

"Lex is nothing if not a gracious hostess." Grady took the beer she handed him. "And it went really well. Lex took over, and she and Katie spent the entire time grooming the horse. By the end, Katie was even helping clean the hooves."

"Smart." Annie closed the dishwasher and twisted the timer. The old machine groaned as it started.

"Yeah. I have to agree with you there. Lex is smart."

"She kind of scares me," Annie admitted.

"She works at that."

"How do you know?"

Grady tipped the beer at her. "If you scare people, they don't try to get too close."

"What makes you such a psychologist?" Annie

folded a dish towel and slipped it through the fridge handle.

"Just a feeling I have."

"About Lex."

He nodded slowly. "About Lex."

GRADY WASN'T CERTAIN exactly when he'd come up with the theory that Lex cultivated a scary persona in an attempt to keep people at bay. At some point since his returning home, the idea had edged into his brain, and the more he thought about it, the more it made sense. He thought back to when he'd first started dating Danielle. Had Lex been scary then? He couldn't decide. She'd been straightforward and no-nonsense. She'd been protective of those she cared about…but had she purposely put people off?

That he didn't know, because she'd been busy protecting Danielle from him and he had a skewed perspective. The situation, he decided, might warrant more investigation. Because he was curious…and he liked the way Lex kissed. But he wanted a real kiss now, not a revenge kiss.

And…he didn't see that happening anytime soon.

Chapter Seven

The boards were all replaced on the damaged side of the barn, and the garage repairs were almost done. Grady was a little further along than he'd thought he'd be at this point—primarily because he'd finally gotten the hang of twin-sitting—and he decided that before he left to catch the first stop of the Bull Extravaganza in late August, he'd build Annie a shed for her gardening equipment. He was also going to build some deep shelves along one of the garage walls so that she could store things more easily.

As it was, the free space in the garage was stacked with plastic bins—those that had survived the wind storm, that is. After the storm, she'd found the girls' baby clothing scattered across a nearby field, and her Christmas decorations had all been destroyed. Despite losses, she still had too many boxed items taking up too much floor space. He'd managed to get a used weight bench crammed into one corner shortly after arriving, but he had to step over boxes to get to it. He was getting tired of boxes.

So…shelving and a shed. When he was done with those projects, it would be time to head out, but this time he was coming back, which meant that he needed to think about where he was going to live during the winter months. Maybe a single-wide mobile home on the edge of the property. The land was half his, after all, and Annie probably wouldn't mind having him around—

"Uncle Grady!"

It was a low-level code-yellow shout. He'd dealt with enough niece emergencies since starting the babysitting gig to know the difference between code red—blood, glass, dangling from a tree limb—and code yellow—salamander loose in the house, accidentally flushed a sneaker, the dishwasher making funny noises.

"Coming."

He rounded the corner of the house and found himself facing two very muddy girls standing on the back porch. They were caked from head to toe.

"Can you carry us into the bathroom so that we don't get mud on the floor?"

"Oh, yeah. So much better to get mud all over me." One edge of his mouth quirked. "How'd you get so muddy?"

Katie pointed at Kristen. "She started it."

"Mom said to share, and you weren't."

"Never mind." Grady blew out a breath. "We'd better get these clothes hosed off before your mom gets home. In fact…how do you feel about a little cold water on a hot day?"

The girls exchanged looks, then shrugged in unison.

Grady set the sprinkler in the middle of the yard and cranked on the water. "Get the mud off and I'll go start the bath."

"Don't forget to put the flower-smelling stuff in the

water," Katie called before racing toward the sprinkler and squealing as she ran through. Kristen followed, and Grady went into the house feeling like a winner. Problem solved and no grit in the bottom of the washer as there'd been the last time the girls had a muddy adventure. He'd had a heck of a time getting the sand out before Annie got home.

After the dripping girls had retired to the bathroom to share a flowery-smelling bath, Grady mopped the water off the floor, congratulated himself on a masterful solution then went out to measure for the shelving. He was getting the hang of this parenthood thing. In fact, he was getting pretty good at it.

On the Monday morning that Danielle left for her Wyoming Wedding Plan Escape with Curtis, Lex got to the store early so that she could do all the things Danielle usually did—arrange flowers, dust the displays, make certain everything was arranged as charmingly as possible.

She was nervous.

A whole week working in the store alone with Annie. It was her store and Annie was an employee—a warm, easy-to-talk-to employee—but Lex never did well in small places with people for prolonged periods of time. She didn't know Annie that well...and she had a feeling she kind of scared the woman. Normally things like that didn't bother her, but they had a whole week stretching ahead of them. Lex prepared herself for a day or two of awkwardness, only to have Annie burst in through the back door two minutes late with her hair still damp. She set down her bag with a thump.

"I'm so sorry I'm late. Rough morning."

"Ah." Lex gave a quick smile before she continued arranging flowers, although not nearly as artfully as Danielle did it.

"My blow dryer got shanghaied and pressed into service as a way to dry a spot on the sofa where a pitcher of water got spilled. Burned the motor out."

"Where was Grady?" Lex asked.

"That *was* Grady."

The ice was officially broken.

She and Annie didn't talk about Grady after that—although Lex had him on her mind. Instead they cautiously broached other topics—high school, the upcoming Founder's Day celebration, their observations about various people in town. They didn't engage in flagrant gossip as Lex and Danielle did, but they edged close enough that Lex decided that she and Annie were on the same page for the most part.

That evening, Grady brought Katie for another Daphne session. The little girl helped Lex groom the mare again, diving in with more enthusiasm this time and feeling comfortable enough to help tie the ribbon in the mare's tail while Lex held it for her.

"Ready to help me saddle?"

"I guess," Katie replied tentatively. Saddling was obviously the next step toward riding, and that was Katie's bugaboo.

Lex knelt in front of the girl, putting herself at eye level. "Here's the thing…horses can sense what we're feeling. If you're confident, then the horse will feel confident, too."

"What's conf-dent?"

"Brave."

Katie's forehead knitted. "If I'm brave, then the horse feels brave."

"You're the leader, not the horse. Horses like being told what to do. It's the way things are when they live wild in herds."

"I'm the horse boss?"

"You are—with a good horse, anyway. There are some horses that'll test you, but with horses like Daphne, yes, you are boss."

"Huh." Katie kicked the gravel at her feet as she considered this new information.

Lex chanced a look at Grady, who was close enough to hear but had remained silent during the exchange. She'd half expected him to chime in, but he didn't. In fact, his expression bordered on unreadable. She told herself she was fine with that, but in all honesty, she liked knowing what Grady was thinking, where his thoughts were. It allowed her to shore up her defenses where needed and plan strategy.

"Shall we saddle?" she asked Katie.

"Okay."

Together, they saddled the horse, Katie helping as much as she could, despite her height disadvantage. Once the saddle was cinched, Lex showed Katie how to lead the horse so that she didn't have to keep looking over her shoulder to make certain she wasn't about to be trod upon.

"I don't think Daphne would step on me," Katie announced, and Grady found himself smiling.

"Not on purpose," Lex agreed. After unsaddling the horse, she asked Katie if she'd like to sit on Daphne's bare back.

Katie looked uncertain at first, but then she nodded.

"I'm the boss," she whispered to herself as Lex helped her up onto the mare's back. Katie clutched the beribboned mane as Daphne let out an equine sigh and cocked a hoof.

"Uh-oh," Lex said. "She's going to sleep."

"That's okay," Katie assured her.

"Okay, now lean forward and give Daphne's neck a hug while she's falling asleep."

"All right." The girl gave the mare a mighty hug.

"Now sit up…" She waited. "…and turn to touch the top of her tail with your right hand…okay, the left hand," she amended as Katie twisted the wrong way. "Now the other hand."

Lex talked the girl through leaning forward to hug the mare's neck again, turning to touch the tail with either hand, then finally, with a little help, leaning back and resting her head on the rump.

"Now, don't you go to sleep," Lex said, and the little girl managed a strangled giggle as she lay stretched out on the horse's back, her little legs at a forty-five-degree angle to the ground.

Katie lifted up from that maneuver, her face red with exertion, then with Lex's help did toe touches and windmills. She slid off the horse, then allowed herself to be tossed back on. All the while Daphne stood and quietly waited for the gymnastic session on her back to end, and Grady watched silently from the fence.

"Good work," Lex said as Katie finally led the mare to the pasture. "How do you feel?"

"More like the boss."

Lex laughed, met Grady's unreadable expression and the laughter died in her throat. She wasn't certain she liked the intense way he was watching her. A few minutes later, after stowing the halter, they headed to the house for Kool-Aid—red today, even though it wasn't Katie's favorite.

Grady didn't have a lot to say, but he drank his Kool-Aid and complimented his niece on her balance. Lex walked with them as far as the front yard gate when it was time for them to go.

"Tomorrow?" she said, brushing aside the hair that had blown across her face.

Katie nodded and Grady settled his hand on the back of his niece's neck. She felt the strong urge to ask him what had made him appear so thoughtful that evening, but decided that (a) it was best not to show interest in his thought processes, and (b) she might not want to know.

"Tomorrow would be great. See you." Then he smiled, and Lex felt her breath catch a little. She lifted her chin, gave a quick nod and headed back to the house.

GRADY BOUGHT THE materials he needed to build the gardening shed on Wednesday morning and had already dug most of the foundation by the time Annie got home. As he'd expected, she'd protested, then beamed at the thought of having a place for her tools. He was going to hold off presenting her with the rototiller he'd decided she needed until he was ready to pull out at the end of the summer. Annie had never been good at receiving gifts. She needed to get better at it.

While Annie dished up stew he'd made in the slow cooker, Grady took a quick shower, washing off the sweat and dirt from the day's digging. He and Katie ate, and then the two of them headed out to Lex's.

He'd be lying if he said he wasn't looking forward to the lesson. Lex was a natural with his niece, showing a side he'd never seen…perhaps never even suspected existed. An intuitive, empathetic side. He'd been fascinated watching her during the last lesson, but he knew better than to show it. So he'd leaned on the fence, the setting sun at his back, figuring she wouldn't be able to read him while squinting into the glare. He planned to do the same tonight. To what end, he didn't know, but he was starting to find Lex interesting in a way he hadn't before.

Lex shot him one quick look as he got out of the truck, then focused solely on Katie, who led the way in the grooming. After bridling the horse, she tossed Katie on top, then put her through the exercises, seeming to know exactly when to put out a reassuring hand and when to let Katie find her own balance. After that, they saddled the horse and once again she helped Katie onto the mare's back.

"Do you think you can do your exercises at a walk if your uncle is beside you?"

Katie sent an alarmed look his way, then tucked her chin against her chest as she debated. "I can try. If Uncle Grady is there. Really close."

"I'll be super close," he said as he climbed through the fence. His gaze connected with Lex's, but all she did was to raise her eyebrows.

"Grab the horn and we'll walk slowly in a circle. And then when you're ready, I'll tell you what to do."

"Okay."

"Remember who's boss," Grady said, smiling up at her.

"All right, Katie, see if you can let go of the horn and ride with your hands out to the side...."

Kate went through all the movements with only a minor amount of help from him. The sun went down, but Katie was doing so well they continued on. Eventually she took the reins and rode Daphne around the edge of the arena, turned her and stopped her and then, wonder of wonders, she trotted. And she smiled as she bounced along on top of the mare, clutching the saddle horn with one hand.

When she stopped, Lex said, "You, my dear, are officially caught up with the other kids, if not past them."

Katie's eye went wide. "But I'm the worst one."

"There is no worst one," Lex said. "Only people progressing at their own speed."

Katie considered her words as she helped put the tack away. "I'm going to tell Kristen that when she complains that she can't draw."

"Excellent plan," Grady said. He waited until Katie headed up the walk to say, "You've done a great job with her."

"Is that it? Lessons are done?" she asked mildly.

"We can't come by on Thursday," he said, wondering if she perhaps wanted to continue. "I have to do some practice rides at Hennessey's, and I'm coaching a couple of kids there."

"I hope it goes better than last time." There was a soft smirk on her face. An expression that was rapidly growing on him.

"Which part?" he asked on an air of innocence. "The part in the arena or the part in the parking lot?"

"Both." She cocked an eyebrow and waited for his response.

"Ouch." He smiled at her.

"Okay," she relented. "The ride wasn't that bad."

"Double ouch." It was the perfect opening to prove that he could do better…but it wasn't the time. As much as he wanted to lean down and kiss her sexy lips, he was going to follow his gut, which said, *If you don't want to blow things, wait.*

"I'll be home late anyway," she said, stopping at the gate and slipping her hands into her back pockets. "We're getting ready for our Fourth of July sale." A thought occurred to her then. "If you're bull riding, who's babysitting?"

"Annie's regular sitter."

"Annie could bring the girls to the store, since it's after hours."

"I'll tell her, but honestly?" He wrinkled his forehead. "It might be better for the store to have them at Emily's house."

Lex smiled at that, and Grady thought that he kind of liked making her smile.

"Maybe we could come for a lesson next week, if you have time."

"I wouldn't mind. You could bring Kristen, too."

"You do understand that one kid is one kid and two kids are four, right?"

Another smile and Grady decided not to push his luck and try for a third. He held out his hand, "Come on, Katie. We'd better get home."

Because he wanted to leave a winner.

LEX FOUND HERSELF thinking about Grady more often then she felt comfortable with. He pushed his way into her thoughts and she had a heck of a time pushing him

back out again. But she managed to get the job done…
usually. Working with Annie added complications to
the matter: how was she supposed to forget the brother
existed while working with his sister?

But she liked Annie and felt comfortable with her,
something that didn't happen all that often with Lex.
They unpacked stock on Friday morning and prepared
for the Fourth of July sale, which was to start on Monday. They had a steady stream of customers and Annie
mentioned that she was half-afraid they wouldn't have
enough stock to put on sale.

"I love the stuff you make," she said as she rear-
ranged the jewelry after two older women made a grat-
ifyingly large purchase in preparation for Christmas,
a mere six months away. She gave a small sigh as she
set down the copper charm bracelet and then picked
up a cowboy boot–shaped brooch. "You are talented."

"My dad taught me," she replied simply. And those
had been good times, just her and him in the basement
workshop, sawing silver sheet metal with the handsaw
and then drawing the designs for her father to etch by
hand. She'd since bought an electric etcher, but every
now and again, she got out the hand tools and tried her
luck at scrollwork. She'd never be as good as Dad, but
trying made her feel closer to him.

"You all have talents." Annie tilted her head as she
picked up the edge of Danielle's grandmother's hand-
tatted tablecloth. "And you all contribute."

Lex shrugged, uncertain what to say. Finally she
said, "How would you have time to indulge in a
hobby?"

"Good point. But I want to learn to do something."

She set down the tablecloth and smiled as the door opened and an elderly man walked in.

"I'm looking for a piece of jewelry for my wife's birthday. Something elegant, but with a Western flavor."

"I think I can help you," Annie said, guiding the man toward the sterling and coral pieces Lex had brought in earlier that month. "These are all handcrafted and one of a kind…"

The man walked out ten minutes later, pleased with the stylized running horse brooch. And Annie thought she had no talents. She was a wonder in the shop, helping customers, working through her lunch hour to rearrange stock. She never seemed to stop, which made Lex wonder if it was a habit born from being a single mother of twins.

"Hey," Lex said as they closed up shop, "would you like to go to Shardlow's for a glass of wine? You know…relax a little before you head back to your other full-time job? It is Friday, after all."

Annie smiled and shook her head. "Thanks, but I have to get home. It's not fair to saddle Grady with the twins for too long."

"I understand." She didn't agree, but she understood. Mother duties came first.

Annie got as far as the door before she turned back. "I might call him. If there are no emergencies and if the girls don't have him operating on his last nerve."

"Or if he doesn't have the girls operating on their last nerves…"

Annie smiled, her eyes crinkling at the corners in a way that reminded her of Grady. She'd never noticed that about Annie before. Was it because the woman didn't smile around her all that much? Or because she'd become ridiculously aware of Grady and the nuances of his expressions?

The latter, she feared, which made her stomach tighten. If she continued on this path, she was on the way to becoming yet another bull rider groupie.

A moment later Annie ended her call. "Grady made a slow-cooker dinner, so I'm free to come home anytime."

"Must be nice to have help around the place." Lex locked the shop door as she spoke.

"Nicer than I imagined. I mean, beyond getting the wind damage fixed and a lot of little things around the house taken care of, it's nice for the girls to get to know their uncle. Frankly it's nice to have company."

It was the "nice for the girls to get to know their uncle" portion of Annie's statement that caught in Lex's brain. Grady hadn't been around enough to really get to know his nieces prior to coming home to help with the tornado damage, and she needed to remember that as she was being sucked in by his charm. Annie could have used some help over the years he'd been gone, and Danielle definitely could have used a partner, yet Grady had essentially walked away from both of them to ride bulls.

"How long will he stay?" The words came out of Lex's mouth almost before they formed in her mind.

"He plans on doing some events in the fall and early winter, but he's too far out of the money now to make finals."

"Events?"

"More exhibitions than real competitions. They usually have them in the bigger cities. Bull versus cowboy. That type of thing. Grady's something of a crowd pleaser."

They went in through the back door of Shardlow's, and Lex reminded herself that she was doing this to break the ice between her and Annie, not to rag on Grady. "I can see that. He's…charming."

Annie gave her an odd look, then pulled out a chair and sat. The barkeep arrived immediately and they both ordered wine. Then Annie propped her elbows on the table and said, "Do you really think Grady is charming?"

It appeared to be a loaded question. "Do you mean am I personally charmed?" As opposed to being aware that he easily charmed other people?

"Yes. That."

Lex considered her next move. To protest too much would be telling—in fact, debating about her response was telling—so she said as honestly and as quickly as possible, "Grady's charm is insidious."

Annie gave a surprised laugh, her eyes once again crinkling at the corners like Grady's. "That's good. And accurate. His charm is insidious, and it got him out of a lot of trouble as a kid."

"Yeah?" Now Lex was leaning forward. She moved back briefly as the barkeep set two glasses of wine, one red, one white, on the table, then leaned forward again.

"I bet you have stories."

"Oh, yes. Many stories." Annie took a sip of wine. "Unfortunately, I've been sworn to secrecy."

Lex laughed even while she was tamping down her disappointment.

"So tell me," Annie said slowly. "Do you get lonely, living by yourself on your farm?"

Lex opened her mouth to say *no*, then stopped. "After my dad died the place was beyond lonely, but I had nowhere else to go." Her fingers curled around the stem of her wineglass. "I couldn't imagine going anywhere else, really." She met Annie's gaze. "So, when you start out lonely, how do you know when you've moved past it?"

"Grady said you have a lot of animals."

"I do."

"Grady used to do that, too. Collect strays."

"Are you sworn to secrecy about that, too?"

"No. I believe these stories are fair game. Suffice it to say that if there was a stray anything in a ten-mile radius, it found its way to our door. Drove Mom crazy, because we were on a very fixed income. Grady used to do chores for the neighbors to help pay for the dog food. And chicken scratch."

"Chickens?"

"We had neighbors—urbanites who were trying out the rural life—who weren't taking care of their flock, so Grady asked to buy them. They became Grady's chickens."

"Grady rescued chickens."

"It was nice having the eggs," Annie said, leaning back in the chair, obviously relaxing for the first time since they went on shift together on Monday morning.

Lex laughed and she, too, felt as if she was relaxing a little. The wine? Or sharing a moment with a new friend? She wasn't sure, but it did feel good to be somewhere other than the farm and the store.

LEX HELD DOWN the fort at the store the next day after insisting that Annie actually take a lunch break. While she was gone, Tiffani Crenshaw, owner of a salon two doors down, came in, browsing the jewelry.

"So, what is going on between you and Grady?" she asked as she held up a rhinestone and crystal necklace. "I see his truck parked at your place almost every night when I drive by."

It was one thing for Danielle to ask what was going on—a whole other thing to have a nosy person who didn't particularly like Lex to ask. Particularly in that catty voice of hers.

"I'm sleeping with him, of course."

"Excuse me?" Tiffani's eyes bulged a little as her head snapped around.

Lex made her expression as innocent as possible. "It's what you assumed, right?" *Or did you simply want to toss out innuendos and watch me squirm?*

"It was just an innocent question," Tiffani sputtered.

Yeah. Right. Tiffani Crenshaw didn't ask innocent questions. She dug for information and then passed it along. But she was also a customer, and Lex had let her irritation get the better of her judgment.

"I was only having some fun with you," Lex said in a placating voice, deciding it would be best if she made a stab at damage control. "I'm giving his niece riding lessons."

"She is," Annie said, stepping out from the back room through the beaded curtains. She beamed at Tiffani, then said, "By the way, we're going to mark down some of the jewelry you were looking at last week. We can give you the sale price a day early if you're interested."

If there was one thing Tiffani loved almost as much

as gossip, it was a good deal, so off she went with Annie, casting a single dark look over her shoulder at Lex.

When Annie came back, Lex said, "You were not supposed to hear that."

"I know you're not sleeping with him."

Lex shifted a little. "I wanted to shut her up. She's so—"

"Toxic?"

"Yes," Lex said with a sudden smile. "Like a nuclear waste dump site." She shook her head and picked up a T-shirt to refold it. "I don't think Danielle will be thrilled with my customer relations."

"Tiffani will be back. She's addicted to sparkles, and you guys have some of the best bling in town."

The bell over the door rang, and three women walked in. Lex excused herself to go to the back room, and once there, she leaned her palms on the antique business meeting table and let her head drop. There were ill-advised ways to handle a touchy situation, and then there were crazy ways. Engaging Tiffani Crenshaw was the latter.

Ever since Grady came back to town, her world had been off-kilter and she'd had just about enough of it. Once Katie was done with lessons, well, she was done with Grady.

She had to be, for her own peace of mind.

Chapter Eight

On Saturday, Grady and his nieces showed up at the fairgrounds shortly after Lex had delivered her horses to the helpers to saddle. She'd planned to unhitch her trailer and run errands but got caught up in a conversation and before she had a chance to unhitch, Katie caught sight of her, waving proudly from atop Daphne. And then the little girl kept checking to see if Lex was still watching her. What could she do but stay?

Abandoning errands, Lex once again found a seat in the stands so that she could watch Katie. Grady had spent the previous lesson leaning on the fence, chatting with a small group of parents and staying close by in case Katie needed him—which she had—but, of course, that was too much to ask for this week. He spotted Lex and made his way toward the stands just as he had during the first lesson. As he climbed toward her, one of the moms shaded her eyes and nudged the woman next to her. Lex lifted a hand to wave at the woman, who weakly waved back and turned away.

Take that, nosy lady.

"What's going on?" Grady asked as he sat next to her.

"People are watching us."

"Whose fault is that?"

"Yours."

"I don't recall initiating any public displays of affection."

"It wasn't affection," Lex said mildly.

"Lust? Public display of lust?"

She tipped her sunglasses down. "Must you?"

One corner of his mouth tipped up wickedly. "Oh, yeah. I must."

She put her sunglasses back in place and made a show of looking through him as if he weren't there. But she was more than aware he was there. She could practically feel the heat from his body. Or maybe it was her body. Whatever, it was disconcerting, but she couldn't bring herself to walk away. Mainly because people were indeed watching them.

Grady leaned back against the seats behind him, the picture of relaxation. "The problem with having been so open about your dislike of me and your disapproval of what transpired between me and Danielle is that it makes our current situation more interesting to onlookers."

"We have no current situation."

"Other than you helping Katie, of course." He directed his gaze back to the arena, where Katie was now slowly jogging along on Daphne, looking a touch nervous, but no more so than many of the other kids. "You really helped her confidence."

"Stop bringing your niece into this."

"I'm not sure what 'this' is."

"Exactly," she said from between clenched teeth. "There is no 'this.'"

The playful expression left his face, and she found

herself staring into a set of very serious gray eyes. "That's where you're wrong."

"How so?" she said on a mock sigh, but inwardly she was in panic mode. Could he read her that easily? Could he tell that being near him was making every nerve in her body go on high alert?

"I heard you said that we're sleeping together."

"I did not!" Her mouth pressed into a flat line and then she said, "Well… I did, but I didn't mean it. I was being facetious. Your sister was there, for Pete's sake." She was going to murder Tiffani Crenshaw.

It was Grady's turn to stare coolly at her. "I'll do some damage control," she muttered.

He scoffed.

"Fine. We'll do nothing. After enough nothing, people will realize that we don't have a relationship."

"I'm still working on why you'd facetiously tell someone we're sleeping together."

"Tiffani Crenshaw wanted to know why your truck was parked at my house every afternoon, and I wanted to shock her into shutting up."

"Well, I guess that backfired." He glanced over at her. "No chance that what you told her was wishful thinking?"

She rolled her eyes and then focused back on the arena. "Right. I lay awake nights thinking about it." Which was kind of true, so she felt mildly uncomfortable saying the words out loud.

A brief silence followed, and she hoped that he would drop the conversation—or at the very least change topics. If he didn't, then she would.

"Hey, Lex?" She turned to find him closer than she expected. Her eyes widened behind the sunglasses, but when he leaned toward her, she didn't lean back. Not even when she knew what was coming. Not when he cupped her cheek with his palm, not when he slowly settled his mouth over hers. Nope. She didn't do one blessed thing to keep him from kissing her. She told herself it was because he wasn't going to cause her to lose her cool, but the truth was, audience or not, she wanted to find out if he tasted as amazing as she'd remembered.

He did and for a few heady seconds, she was lost. Grady Owen could kiss, could make her abandon her sense of the here and now and simply lose herself. Forget who he was. Heck, she almost forgot who she was. A split second later, when his hand traveled from her face down to her hip, she snapped to her senses, put her palms on his chest and pushed.

"That's it." Lex got to her feet, forgetting about not losing her cool. "I'm not engaging in a spectator sport."

Grady looked surprised. "It's okay if you do it, but not if I do it?"

"There are children present."

"They aren't looking."

Sure enough, they were all totally focused on Jared.

"Fine. There are gossipy parents present, and they are looking." Every single one of them. And they looked away as one, focusing on the arena when she started marching down the steps.

"Since when," he called, "do you care what anyone thinks?"

She stopped dead, turned back. "You don't know what I care about. What I don't."

"Maybe I'd like to know more." He sounded serious, which only made her feel more panicked.

She gave a loud snort. "*That* is not going to happen."

And this was the last time she was going to let her hormones overrule her head. She had the answer to her question. He was an amazing kisser. Information stored away, no need to repeat.

She stomped down off the bleachers, continued the walk of shame to her trailer then decided, screw it. The sooner she faced things, meaning the interested bystanders, the better. She took a couple of cleansing breaths, then headed over to the group of parents, pasting a smile of sorts on her face, doing her best to ignore the fact that her lips felt swollen.

"Hi, Frank. Gloria." The owners of an insurance business, who'd graduated high school with her. She didn't know the other parents that well, but had a feeling that Frank and Gloria had filled them in on her history with Grady. "Are your kids enjoying lessons?"

"I'm now being hounded night and day to buy a horse." Frank gave his wife a small nudge. "We're *so* glad we signed them up, right, honey?"

"Lessons and horses have been the topic of conversation for the past week," Gloria agreed. "Tiffani says you give private lessons." She smiled at Lex in a way that was half amused and half congratulatory.

Lex lifted her chin. "Annie Owens works for me, so I gave one of her twins extra help this week." It was now difficult to tell the sisters apart by posture, and despite being totally irritated at the situation, Lex felt a small upwelling of pride. "It was a favor to Annie, not official lessons."

Gloria glanced over at Grady sitting alone in the stands. "So your lessons aren't going to…continue?"

The other parents smiled at the innuendo, and Lex

felt herself start to slide into defense mode. She'd had enough double-talk and was about to set the record straight in no uncertain terms when she realized that would be really hard to do when Grady had just kissed her in the stands. *Leave it be. Walk away.* That would be the sensible thing, but she couldn't help addressing the topic directly. "Are you talking about me and Grady or me and the twins?" she asked in a conversation-stopping voice.

"You and Grady," Gloria said, totally unabashed. "I think you're cute together."

Lex blinked at her. What was she supposed to say to that?

"Fireworks make for an interesting relationship," Frank added. The woman standing next to him nodded her agreement.

Lex simply stared at the small group of parents as she realized that Grady had been 100 percent correct when he predicted that there was no such thing as damage control in this situation.

"Glad you think so," she finally said to no one in particular. "Now, if you'll excuse me, I need to shovel out my horse trailer."

GRADY WAS OF the opinion that he needed to come up with a way to kiss Lex again under better circumstances. If a ten-second kiss was that good, what would it be like if they had, say, thirty seconds…or a couple of minutes…or the entire night?

Probably not something he should dwell on as he drove his nieces home, but it was hard not to.

He didn't think Lex was immune to him. Not when she kissed him back as she had tonight. What she was,

was overly self-protective. And maybe torn, because while she purported to dislike and disapprove of him, she'd also started a rumor about them—a rumor that he wouldn't mind turning into reality.

But if they did make it reality, Lex's heart had to be in it. She couldn't be doing it to make a point or win a battle or something. That would be wrong… and he didn't think Lex was the kind to sleep with him for those reasons. She was too honest. With him, anyway. Sometimes he wondered how honest she was with herself. Whatever, the situation left Grady teetering on the edge of frustration…but it also kept the summer interesting.

When they got to the house, the girls dove into their reading. They had until Monday to read the last book of the required twenty that were necessary to receive reading awards from the mayor and partake in the ice cream party and pool party that followed. Annie told him that the contest had become quite a big deal in the town, and because of the grant money received, they were able to give bigger and better prizes each year. This year the names of all the kids who qualified would go into a draw for a bicycle.

What impressed Grady most, though, was that the contest was on the honor system and the girls never once considered skimming a book. Instead they were scrupulously honest, reading every word of every book, before asking him or Annie to sign the paper where they'd recorded title and author.

"I love how earnest they are," he said after Katie had carefully placed her signature paper in a plastic folder before heading back to the bedroom where Kristen was still reading.

"I know. Too bad people can't hang on to that." Annie refolded the afghan that lay over the arm of a recliner that had seen better days, then took a seat.

"I think we do hang on to it," Grady said as he picked up the television remote more out of habit than anything, "but it gets buried under all the other baggage we stack on top of it. We lose sight of it."

Annie shot him a look. And then she kept looking at him.

"What?"

"That was insightful."

"Why does that surprise you?" He wondered if he should be amused or insulted. He started clicking through the muted television channels.

"Because you put on that cocky bull rider act most of the time."

He paused on a sports channel, not bothering to look up as he said, "It's not an act. I'm that good."

"You're full of—"

"Hey, Mom?" Kristen came into the room, holding two dresses on hangers, one pale yellow and the other a turquoise and brown polka-dot print.

"You were saying?" Grady asked innocently.

"I think you can fill in the blank." Annie turned to her daughter, and they conferred on which dress was more mayor worthy. Grady noted that she picked the one that would be least likely to show chocolate syrup later—something he wouldn't have noticed a mere two months ago.

Annie settled back in her chair, watching the silent television as Grady continued to flip channels. If he found something worthwhile, he'd turn on the sound.

"Quite the rumor going around town about you and Lex."

Grady's finger stuttered on the remote. Boom, out with the big guns. "The one Tiffani is spreading?" he asked blandly.

Annie shook her head. "No. I was there when that happened. This one involves the grandstands at the riding lessons." She sent him a look of mock concern. "Do you really think you should be making out in the stands while my daughters are present?"

"They weren't looking."

"Everyone else was."

Exactly what Lex had said. And she'd been right. And he didn't regret kissing her one bit.

Grady propped one foot up on the worn ottoman. There really was no fighting this. Not as long as he and Lex continued to spar—and kiss—in public. "You want to hear a secret, Annie?"

"I'm all about secrets."

"I like Lex." Her eyebrows slowly lifted at his casual confession. He rather enjoyed that, even though the frustration caused by the Lex situation was once again taking hold. "I can't say that the feeling is mutual, or that anything will come of it, but...I like her." He spoke with simple sincerity because that was the way things were.

Annie gave a considering nod as she casually twisted the fringe on the afghan through her fingers. "So *that's* why you keep kissing her. Now it all makes sense."

"She kissed me first," he pointed out.

"To make a point. Right. I forgot."

Grady smiled at the irony in his sister's voice, even

though he no longer felt like smiling. The conversation drove home the point that he had a problem. This was no longer about winning or losing some battle of wills or saving face or anything like that. It was about being attracted to a woman who could erect a barrier faster than most people could sneeze—which was why it was possible nothing would come of the fact that he found himself more and more drawn to her.

Despite that, he felt a deep need to test the waters. The big question was how.

"Well, you did tell Tiffani you were sleeping together," Danielle said as she and Lex flipped through racks of bridesmaid dresses. Great-granny hadn't made the trip and Danielle's mother and grandmother were one rack over, so they could finally talk. Lex wouldn't have talked at all if Danielle hadn't gotten wind of the story just before they left for Bozeman that morning and asked if it was true. That had opened the floodgates of Lex's frustration at being part of a public spectacle. It would have been one thing if there really was something between them, but there wasn't.

"I was making a point to her," Lex said from between her teeth. They'd been conversing in snatches for the past hour whenever they managed to get away from the older Perry women. "To make her realize she was sticking her nose where it didn't belong."

"Didn't seem to work."

"Tell me about it."

Danielle turned to Lex, still holding the skirt of a pale yellow dress, even though her dresses were supposed to be pink. "What do you have against Grady?"

"Oh, let's see. Maybe the fact that he chose rodeo

over you?" How could Lex not hold that against him? He'd seriously talked marriage with a woman who couldn't handle his career. He shouldn't have done that—not when he hadn't been willing to give up the career.

"Let me clarify. What do *you* have against him?"

Lex had no answer for that, so she pulled a rose pink minidress off the rack and held it out, more to look busy than because she thought it was a possibility.

"No!" Danielle's mother called from across the store, and Lex instantly put it back.

"In case you didn't know," she said without looking at Danielle, "track records matter."

"People change."

Lex gave her head a shake, as if trying to clear it. "What are you saying?"

"People. Change."

"No. Are you saying that I should have something to...do...with Grady?"

"He has his good points."

"Along with a few character flaws."

"Who doesn't? All I'm saying is don't dislike him just because you think you should. Because of me."

"He didn't do his sister any favors by never coming home."

"He's home now."

Lex pulled in a breath. "Please don't tell me again that people change." Fortunately Danielle couldn't have if she'd wanted to, because her grandmother had given an excited shout from nearby and then proudly displayed the *perfect* bridesmaid dress...if one were a sugarplum fairy.

Lex left Danielle to tactfully deal with the tulle and

satin dilemma and concentrated on putting their conversation out of her head. She had reasons for her feelings about Grady, and no one was going to talk her out of them. Just as she hadn't allowed people to talk her out of being friends with some of the less-than-cool kids in high school. Lex followed her heart and her head. Only her hormones seemed to get her into trouble, so they were out of the equation.

After Danielle had explained to her grandmother that she was looking for something a little sleeker and got the sparkly puffy dress safely back on the rack, the team broke for lunch.

"Next we'll go to Carson's Wedding Boutique," Mrs. Perry announced happily. "That'll be the most likely place to find the perfect dress for Danielle."

At least all of Danielle's relatives had gotten over the disappointment of her not choosing a family dress to restyle, and all were now focused on the hunt for the perfect wedding dress with which to torture some future granddaughter.

Twenty minutes later, Lex was idly perusing the display racks while Danielle changed into her first choice and her mother and grandmother waited, seated in white leather chairs with glasses of sparkling water in their hands. Lex couldn't make herself sit still.

This situation with Grady was bugging the heck out of her. How had everyone gotten the idea that they were an item? A couple of kisses? Who didn't kiss a casual date good night? Did that make them a couple?

"Try this."

Lex turned to find an associate standing behind her, holding a draped column of a dress with no embellishments other than a few artfully crafted fabric roses on one side of the neckline. She swept it through the air to hold it up to Lex before she could utter a word of protest. The silk charmeuse whispered over her skin and she could see that the skirt was deceptively full, even though it was cut to cling to the hips.

"Very 1930s," the woman explained. "Perfect for your figure."

"I'm not the bride," Lex said.

"Oh." The dress drooped a little; then the woman lifted the hanger again. "You will be, and when you are, you need to remember this dress. Perfect, perfect, perfect."

"Thank you," Lex said, and then she was saved by Danielle making her way out of the dressing room, looking stunning in a simple satin gown.

"You're both lucky women," the associate murmured. "You don't need a lot of glitter and glitz, because you have presence."

"Thank you," Lex murmured again, thinking that the woman was good. Because at that moment, thanks to her, she did feel as if she had presence, and there was no question that Danielle had it. It felt odd being placed in the same category as her friend, who was a bona fide knockout.

"This dress is perfect," Danielle said, turning in front of the mirror as the associate pinched the fabric here and there, showing where it could be altered.

Perfect dress or not, she tried on seven more at her mother's behest before they decided that the first one was indeed *the one*. By the time the alteration card had been filled out, Lex would have loved a pitcher of beer, but instead she made do with a small glass of red wine at the victory dinner before heading back to Gavin.

"You know," Lex said after dropping off Danielle's mother and grandmother, "I don't think this dress will be all that bad if your daughter wanted to wear it."

"We say that now," Danielle said with a wide smile. The smile faltered a little and she said, "About our earlier conversation… Grady and such…" Lex sucked in a fortifying breath, but all her friend said was, "…We won't talk about that again. I can see that it isn't your favorite topic."

That was why Danielle was her best friend. She let her off the hook when she really needed to get off the hook. Right now she didn't even want to think about Grady Owen. She simply wanted to get on with her life, such as it was.

Lex got home to find a message on her landline message machine and, curious about whom on earth would be calling the landline, pushed the play button.

"Hi, Alexa. This is Pete. I couldn't help noticing that you had a lot of animals at your place and wondered if you might be able to foster a flock of ducks as a favor to me. Call me if you haven't already hung up. Thanks." Lex smiled to herself as she jotted down his number and then called him back.

"Why do you need a foster home for ducks?"

"It's a long story, but my grandmother recently sold her house and is moving. There will be a two-month period in which she will have no home, so she's going to Minnesota to stay with her sister."

"Okay…"

"The ducks are a special breed. Exotic something or others."

"Something or others?"

"Waterfowl aren't my thing," he confessed. "They come with a pool and a pen and everything."

"How many?"

"Six."

"What if something happens to them?"

"It's on me...so if you think something's going to happen to them, say no."

"I have a cat and three dogs, but they never bothered my chickens when I had them, so... I guess."

"Thank you, Alexa. I'll be in touch."

"You're welcome."

She hung up without saying, *"How hard could duck-sitting be?"* because she'd learned the hard way that nothing ruined a day like taunting the cosmos. And one thing about the ducks—they took her mind off Grady for almost a minute or two.

Chapter Nine

The day of the Dedicated Reader Awards and ice cream pig-out dawned sunny and clear. Annie laid out a battle plan. Grady would bring the girls to Jaycee Park, arriving early so that Annie could make certain they still looked presentable. She'd save him a seat in the parents' section. After the fun was over, he'd take the girls home and quite possibly make prodigious use of the stain removal prewash spray.

"Okay, so the girls are ready to go. All you have to do is to get them to the park by eleven. Danielle and I will walk over from work."

Annie was repeating herself, so Grady got the idea that this reading awards ceremony was important to her. As it should be. The girls had read a goodly number of books to qualify for the honor.

"Who'll mind the store?" he said.

Annie smiled. "We're putting up a bee-back-soon sign. Danielle wants to see the girls get their dedicated reader awards, too."

"What about Lex?" Not that he was thinking about her or anything.

"She has something going on this afternoon, or I'm sure she'd be at the awards, too."

"It's cool that this is such a big deal."

"I know. They've made it so that getting the award is a real achievement."

"What's an achievement?" Kristen asked as she came into the kitchen with Katie a few steps behind her.

Annie leaned down to give each girl a kiss. "Your awards. They mean you've accomplished something."

"I got an award for breathing once," Grady said. Annie shot him a dark look, and the girls both cocked their heads. "It was all about self-esteem," he explained. "Everybody got an award just for showing up at basketball camp."

"How's that special?" Kristen asked.

"It isn't. Which is why these awards of yours are real special. You did something hard to earn them. Where do you think my award for breathing is?"

"I don't know."

"Neither do I. But I can tell you exactly where my rodeo buckles, my high school letter and my spelling bee award are."

"You won a spelling bee?"

Grady looked at Annie. "All these scars and buckles and they're impressed by the spelling award."

"As well they should be." Annie gave her girls "the look." "Stay clean."

"We will."

"No mud pies. In fact…don't leave the house."

The girls nodded in unison. Grady had to admit that they looked pretty cute in their dresses, one purple and blue, one turquoise and brown, similar in style but different enough to allow the girls their own personality, and he also knew how quickly they could get uncute, given the proper mix of mud and water.

Once Annie drove away, he jerked his head toward the living room. "Watch television until it's time to leave, okay?" He went into the kitchen and came back with the timer. "If I'm not back in the house when this thing dings, then come and get me, okay?"

"All right." Kristen already had the remote and was cruising through channels while Katie curled up on the opposite end of the sofa, tucking her feet underneath her.

"Stop!" she called. "I want to watch that..."

Grady let himself out the back door, hoping to get at least a start on framing the gardening shed before he had to take off for town.

As he fully expected, he lost track of time. What he hadn't expected was to look at his watch and realize that the girls should have called him twenty minutes ago. If he didn't get a move on, they were going to be late.

He jogged to the house, peeling out of his sweaty T-shirt as he went. "Girls, get whatever you need. We have to go. Now." He disappeared into his room and came out buttoning a light blue long-sleeve shirt. He stepped out onto the porch and quickly brushed the fine sawdust off the jeans that were going to have to do, because he didn't have time to take off his boots and find new ones. When he came back out into the kitchen, there was no sign of the girls...but there were noises coming out of the bathroom. Water splashing noises mixed with hissed whispers.

His stomach clenched as he approached the door. He hesitated, then gave a short rap. There was a gasp on the other side of the door, and then Kristen said, "We need a few more minutes to get ready."

"You were ready."

"Uh…" More water noises. More whispers.

"What's going on?" He rapped again. "Come on. What's going on in there?"

"Nothing."

"I'm counting to three. One…"

The door cracked open. Grady pushed it the rest of the way open, then almost fell over when he saw Katie.

"How?"

It was the only word he could manage. *How* had Katie managed to dye half of her head pink?

The girls shuffled guiltily. "We already got most of it off."

He didn't think so. "What is it?" he asked, coming into the tiny room to get a closer look.

Both girls shrugged. "Something that came with the new cake baking set."

Food coloring perhaps? Two fresh dresses hung from the towel bar, ready to replace the wet ones they were wearing.

Grady did his best to be positive as he freaked out. "Okay, the dresses—that's good, but what about your hair?"

Katie picked up a dripping hank of pink hair and dropped it again. Her lip shook a little; then she sucked it up and said, "I wanted a little pink streak in my hair. My friend Rose's mom let her have a little pink streak for the awards."

"Why didn't you ask your mom to help you?"

"We thought she'd say no," Kristen said. "So I helped, but more came out than was s'posed to."

Better to ask for forgiveness than permission—a strategy he was well familiar with. But neither forgiveness nor permission was going to help them now.

"I…uh…don't know what to do," he admitted to himself out loud as he took a closer look. "A hat maybe?"

"We don't got hats."

"Except for winter ones."

Somehow he didn't think a knit cap was the answer. Desperation jabbed him as he fought for a solution to partially pink, dripping wet hair. She'd gotten a streak all right—one that covered about a third of her head. The top of one ear was pink, too.

"You could braid it," Kristen said, "and hide some of the pink." Katie's face brightened, then fell again as Grady shook his head.

"I'm not talented in that particular arena. Can you braid?" he asked Kristen. She shook her head sadly.

"Lex taught me," Katie said. "But I can't do my own hair yet."

"Well, we've got to do something. We may not be early like your mom asked, but if we can figure something out fast—"

"Mom might not kill us?" Katie asked hopefully.

"I was thinking more along the lines of we won't be that late." Killing was a given at this point.

He walked around his niece, trying to figure out his next move, visualizing what the rodeo girls had taught him to do with his horse's tail while they were flirting with him in high school. Over, under, over…stick in a ribbon. He could do it…or something close to it.

He pulled the new hair dryer off the shelf and clicked it to high as he pointed it at Katie's head. He was probably setting in the color and doing all kinds of wrong, but darn it, they were going to make that ceremony. Once her hair was dry—which thankfully hadn't taken that long—he set the dryer on the back of the toilet and assessed. The pink wasn't a soft petal pink that would have blended with her natural blond— it approached neon. It needed to be hidden.

"Katie, change your dress fast. Kristen, find me a brush and some hair dudes while she changes. Then you go change." Kristen frowned at him and he said, "You know, rubber bands or whatever they're called."

"Elastics," Katie said as she grabbed her dress off the towel bar and headed for the door.

"And some kind of bow," he said to Kristen, who was now rummaging through drawers. "Something really, really big."

LEX GOT BACK from her dental appointment earlier than expected, and while she'd offered to watch the store, she was glad when Danielle insisted on putting up the bee-back-soon sign with the little honey bee on the corner. Several small businesses took time off every year for this event. Thanks to a grant and a dedicated county librarian, the city made a big deal about their reading program. The winners at each grade level received prizes and a special award from the mayor and were then guests of honor at a sundae-making party and the games and prize drawings that followed.

Lex and Danielle and Annie managed to get front-row seats in the parents' section, and Annie stacked all of their purses on Grady's chair. As soon as they were seated, Annie checked her watch, then craned her neck, trying to see the parking lot. "They're supposed to be here by now."

"Maybe Grady lost track of time."

"He better not have. Last year they missed getting Dedicated Reader Awards by only a couple books, and it crushed them." Annie pulled out her phone and started texting.

The chairs were rapidly filling up and soon there were none left except for the one next to Annie, and only two empty chairs on the stage.

The head librarian, Mr. Westcott, took the microphone and welcomed the families and friends of this year's dedicated readers. He explained the program as Annie squirmed in her seat. Next he handed the microphone to the mayor and just as Annie reached in her purse to take her phone out again, Grady's truck roared into the parking lot. Annie's shoulders relaxed and then, as she caught sight of the girls jogging on either side of Grady, they stiffened again. It was pretty obvious why.

One of the twins looked as though she was dressed for an awards ceremony—cute dress, shiny black shoes, curled hair bouncing on her shoulders. The other twin… Katie, maybe?…also had on a cute dress and shiny black shoes. Her hair, however, was twisted up into a bun thing, and balanced in front of the bun was what appeared to be a floral display.

"Oh, dear heavens," Annie said on a low groan.

The girls took their seats behind the mayor, and Grady stepped to the side of the stage, shifting his weight and folding his arms over his chest. He looked relieved and stressed at the same time. And maybe a little afraid. He didn't so much as glance their way.

Lex pressed her lips together, because it was all she could do to keep a straight face when she looked back at Katie. Flowers everywhere. She wouldn't have been surprised to discover that duct tape was involved somewhere in the process.

"She looks adorable," Danielle said, patting Annie's knee.

"I think her hair is pink," Annie responded.

"How can you tell?" Lex asked. It was hard to see her hair with all the flowers.

Awards were given, Katie's hair stayed up for the most part and she only lost two flowers on the way to the podium. Another little girl picked them up and solemnly handed them back as Katie took her seat. Grady stayed where he was, out of harm's way, but Lex didn't think that was going to last for long.

After the mayor announced the award winners, Annie found her girls and hugged them, telling them how proud she was. Even though she gave the pink hair a long, hard look, she didn't say a word as she hugged Katie again, kissed her head and told her to get in line. Then she stood up and zeroed in on her brother, still standing twenty feet away. He made a helpless gesture and started toward them. Lex knew she should leave, but there was no way she was missing out on this explanation.

"I appreciate you babysitting, Grady. Really, I do—"

"She wanted a pink streak in her hair. Like Rose. I had nothing to do with it."

"Somehow she doesn't look like Rose," Annie pointed out.

"She has roses..." Grady smiled weakly.

"That she does." Annie settled her hands on her hips, then let out a sigh. "You get points for creativity."

"I had to duct-tape some of the lower flowers. Hopefully it won't hurt too much when you take them out."

"Of course you duct-taped them." Annie shook her head. "Go have a sundae, Grady."

"Yeah. I'll do that." He started toward the line, where Katie and Kristen were.

"I think he did a decent job," Lex said. Surprisingly she meant it. He must have been horrified to find that he had a neon pink–haired kid on his hands. A laugh welled up inside her, but she choked it back and gave a small cough.

"Yeah," Annie replied. "But it's still a touch embarrassing."

"I'm sure she'll be in the picture they put on the front page of the newspaper," Lex said. The reporter had certainly taken enough photos of her, knowing a human interest story when he saw one.

"No doubt." Annie smiled up at her. "Do you want to get a sundae?"

"No. I'll head back to the shop. Enjoy yourself."

"Thanks."

Before Lex turned to go, Grady caught her eye from where he stood in line between the twins, and she saw something she didn't usually see in his expression. Uncertainty. Good. Guys like Grady needed a little uncertainty in their lives.

THE DUCKS ARRIVED the next day, along with their grateful owner, Peter's grandmother, Nancy, a plump woman in her late seventies who'd at one time been her down-the-road neighbor. Each duck had a name, and Nancy had thoughtfully provided Lex with an identification key. To Lex's untrained eyes, all the female ducks looked the same, both in the labeled photos and in person. The only one she could identify from the photo was Channing, the drake.

"I named him after Channing Tatum," Nancy confided. "I waited a long time to hatch such a perfect specimen."

"Excellent choice," Lex said. "I see the resemblance."

With Peter's help, they set up the pen, made of sections of grid fencing—complete with a protective screen over the top—and the portable pond, which needed to have water running through it all the time to keep it fresh. Then there were food troughs, bags of food, a duck house. When they were done, Lex understood why Peter had called her. Not many people would have had the space for this.

"Only seven weeks," Nancy cooed to the ducks, who seemed more interested in grazing on the fresh green grass than in listening to their mama. Lex's dogs had watched as the pen had been built, showed a moderate amount of interest when the ducks were released then all but yawned and fallen asleep after the ducks settled in. Like Peter, waterfowl were not their thing. Nor were the ducks of interest to Felicity. The cat rubbed against Lex's leg, then headed to the house, tail swaying in the air.

Nancy looked close to tears as she walked toward Peter's truck. She stopped before opening the door and pulled a wallet out of her jacket pocket. "Will thirty dollars a week be enough?"

"For caring for the ducks?" Lex asked in surprise. She shook her head. "I can't take money. It'll be a privilege to keep them for you."

Nancy's face brightened. "Really?"

"Of course. I may have to get some ducks of my own."

"You will never regret it. They bring such joy!"

Lex met Peter's eyes. He smiled at her, a very nice smile from a very handsome guy, and she felt…nothing.

Damn.

Just because Grady sparked something inside her every time she was close to him, just because she thought about their kisses a bit more than she should, it didn't mean she had to obsess or worry. She was in control of her life, not Grady and not the community. She would bring this thing with Grady back to where it should be. Mutual animosity would be nice, but animosity only seemed to encourage him.

And her.

She needed to get a handle on the situation, establish a casual-acquaintance relationship with him and then maybe she could relax. No more kissing—that was a given. She was simply too private a person to be a participant in a spectator sport, and if that meant telling Grady that he had won the war, so be it. She'd happily wave the white flag of surrender.

Chapter Ten

On Monday morning Annie came in to the store looking frazzled. The twins, she explained as she hung up her purse and pulled on the smock she wore at the store, had started coming down with colds on Saturday, were cranky as could be on Sunday and now they were officially sick.

"Do you want to take the day off?" Danielle asked with a concerned frown.

Annie tied the waist strings at the back of the smock. "No. Grady's doing fine with them, but I do need to run the cough medicine out to him before noon. The pharmacist said he'd have the prescription filled by ten. I'd be back in less than an hour."

"Or I could drop it off on my way home," Lex offered, recognizing a golden opportunity when she saw one. She could talk to Grady in relative privacy instead of at riding lessons or some other public forum. "Unless you want to check on the girls, that is."

Annie's expression brightened. "You don't mind? Dropping it off? I mean..." She made a face, and Lex knew what she was thinking. If she didn't mind seeing Grady after becoming the talk of the community by kissing in the stands and telling Tiffani the Mouth that they were sleeping together.

"It's on my way home," Lex repeated matter-of-factly.

"Thanks so much. It actually might be better if you brought it. If the girls are awake when I get there, they may not want me to leave." Annie smiled a little. "They're never clingy except when they get sick. Then it's cuddle city."

Half an hour later Lex turned into Annie's driveway. The garage door was open, and next to the small table saw was a weight bench. Grady was on his back, pressing a big barbell.

Lex got out of the truck and strolled over, white pharmacy bag in hand. "You shouldn't do that without a spotter."

Grady hefted the barbell back into the stand and then sat on the bench, reaching for a towel, which he used to wipe his shoulders and chest. A scar started at his rib cage and dipped south, and Lex noted a few smaller scars scattered here and there. Scars that probably meant he'd barely escaped death. The idea made her stomach tighten. "It won't crush me. I wait for Annie to do the heavy ones."

"Good to know," Lex said briskly, shoving thoughts of near death out of her head and tearing her gaze away from the sheen of perspiration on his incredibly muscled torso. She held up the bag. "Cough medicine."

"Great." He slung the towel around his neck and got to his feet, crossing to stop in front of her, and as soon as he got close, she felt all the sensations she'd convinced herself she wouldn't feel when she was near him. The feeling that she couldn't get quite enough air in her lungs. The tiny electric prickles of awareness dancing over her skin. She lifted her chin, commanded herself to get a grip.

"Have any hair adventures lately?" she asked mildly.

"Nope, and I'm happy to say that while the pink stuff doesn't wash out, it gets lighter as time goes on." Grady took the bag from her as she held it out. The paper rustled as he lowered his hand to his side.

"I told Annie I'd deliver that because it's on my way home," she explained, even though he hadn't asked.

"And you wanted to see me. Straighten out a few things."

She frowned at him, wondering when he'd become so good at reading thoughts. "It needs to be done," she said. "We can't keep entertaining our friends and acquaintances."

"Why not?"

"I don't like it," she responded evenly.

His mouth tilted up on one side into a sensual curve. For a moment she thought he was going to say, *"I beg to differ—you do like it,"* which was an unfortunate truth, but instead he said, "You know… I was trying to figure out the other day how this all got started with me and you. I think it comes down to you taking an instant dislike to me when I started dating Danielle."

"No. I took an instant dislike to you when you chose the PBR over her."

"But you think she's better off now, right?"

She didn't have an answer to that one. One corner of Grady's mouth tipped up as he wiped the towel over his neck. She tore her gaze away and focused on the first thing she could find worthy of comment, as she collected her thoughts and prepared for another volley. "The garage looks a lot better."

"I'm waiting on the siding. Then a little paint and good as new." He pointed to the framed-in building a few yards away. "Annie's new garden shed."

"I had no idea you were into construction."

"There's a lot you don't know about me."

She met his eyes dead-on. "And things will stay that way."

He looked amused. "Is this your way of saying uncle?"

"Yes. Uncle. You win." She held out her hand. "Let's call a truce."

He glanced down at her hand, then took it in his calloused fingers and instead of shaking it, held on to it as he studied her cautiously. "This feels like a trap."

She laughed in spite of herself. "No trap. I'm tired of being watched. Talked about."

"And that's it."

"What else could it be?"

His eyebrows lifted. "I'm not touching that one."

"Because there's nothing to touch," she said through gritted teeth. What was it about this guy that instantly set her off, despite having every intention of maintaining an even keel?

"Yeah. Right."

"Where do you find hats big enough to fit your head?"

"This isn't ego talking."

"I'm done," she said, pulling her hand away yet still feeling the warmth of his fingers on hers.

She turned toward the bay door but only managed a couple of steps before he said, "I think we should go out." She turned back, certain she hadn't heard correctly. "Instead of playing this game." He set his hands on his hips, his weight cocked to one side.

She closed the distance between them in a few short steps, pointing a finger at him. "Maybe you're playing a game. I'm not."

"Yeah you are, and maybe we need to be honest with one another."

"Here's some honesty." She reached out and yanked the damp towel from around his shoulders, trying to startle the calm expression off his face. Why should he feel calm when she didn't? He didn't look massively startled by her unexpected action, but his eyes did narrow a little, so she continued on. "We are not going out. We are not kissing one another. We are going to retreat to our neutral corners and stay there."

She wadded up the towel and jammed it back at him.

"Whatever. If you need me, I'll be in my corner."

"Why would I need you?"

"One thing I've discovered in life, Lex, is that you never know who you might need."

"And that's where you're wrong. I will never need you." She meant it from the core of her being. Because needing Grady would put her in a very vulnerable position, and Lex didn't do vulnerable.

WELL, THAT WENT WELL.

Grady stalked into the house and tossed his towel into the laundry box as he walked into the utility room. He'd taken the plunge, asked her out. He'd been honest. Lex not so much.

He told himself it was because she was threatened.

Scared for some reason, but it was still hard to swallow. She was brave in all other aspects of life...why not this one? Why not take a chance on him? It wasn't as if he'd asked for a huge commitment or anything. A date. One lousy date.

The woman drove him insane.

He pulled a T-shirt out of the dryer and slipped it on. He still had a lot to do today with the siding and the shed, so he'd wait until Annie got home to shower. A raspy cough sounded from the living room, and he went back into the kitchen, where he opened the paper bag Lex had delivered, took out the medication and used his pocketknife to slit the cellophane holding the dosage cup attached to the top of the bottle.

"Uncle Grady?" Katie's call was punctuated by another low cough.

"Coming, kiddo." He walked into the living room, where Katie was curled up on one end of the sofa and Kristen at the other, both covered with handmade afghans. No way were they going to spend downtime in bed, where Annie wanted them to be. They wanted to fall asleep to cartoon shows, and Grady wasn't going to argue with them.

Katie pushed herself upright, her pinkish hair semi-matted on one side of her head. She coughed again and Grady held up the medication and measuring cup. "I got the cure."

She smiled and let him pour the proper dosage, which he checked not once, not twice, but three times, and then she swallowed it. "Cherry," she said with a wrinkle of her nose.

"I don't know if they make blue cough syrup, sweetie."

"You should check," she said as she settled back into her nest and coughed again.

He looked over at Kristen, who was sleeping soundly, her mouth hanging open. When kids slept, they really slept. He wasn't going to wake her up to take medicine. When she needed it, she'd wake up.

"Do you need anything? Water? Crackers?" he asked.

Katie yawned and shook her head, then coughed weakly as she picked up the remote. "No."

"Okay. Well, I'm going to work on your mom's shed some more. If you need me…"

"I know." She pointed at Annie's cell phone, which his sister had sacrificed so that they could call Grady in from outside by merely pressing one button.

She yawned again, and Grady expected her to be sound asleep in a matter of minutes. It was the first time since the cake incident that he'd been absolutely certain of where he'd find the girls when he returned to the house. Tomorrow would probably be a different story, since Annie told him that kids bounced back fast. She'd know, and he was learning.

Funny thing—he really enjoyed pseudoparenthood. Even the pink-haired emergency parts.

That was one good thing he'd gotten out of coming home. And he was enjoying the time with his sister. Two good things. He no longer wondered if he and Danielle were meant to be. Three good things.

And…maybe he'd better stop there while he was ahead. Because if he gave any thought to the Lex matter, he was once again going to start dwelling on the one big negative of his return home. He was falling for a woman who swore she was never going to need him in any way, shape, or form.

LEX WAS BUSILY currying the minidonkeys early Thursday morning when a familiar white utility truck pulled into her driveway and Peter got out of it.

He smiled that easy smile of his as he approached. "My grandmother wanted me to visit the ducks."

Lex laughed as she set down the currycomb and started toward him, the two donkeys and the goat trailing behind her. "They're doing great." She gestured toward the pen. "Come and see for yourself."

They walked to the pen, and then Peter took out his phone, giving her a self-conscious smile. "She wants pictures."

Lex simply smiled back. Peter took a few photos, then pocketed the phone. "They look as happy as ducks can look." Channing waddled by, making a clackety sound with his bill. He looked so serious as he went about his duck business, and the lady ducks did seem to find him incredibly attractive.

"Your grandma was right. I do enjoy them. I sit on the porch and watch them waddle around and swim. Feed them duck treats and veggie peelings. I'd love to let them out and see them in action on the stock pond." Which was what she'd do if she got a small flock of her own. Ducks on the pond would be nice. Of course, she was going to get the not-so-exotic kind. Regular ducks were good enough for her.

"These guys will never taste freedom," Peter said with a half smile. "Gram is too nervous about their safety. She hatched them all, you know. Raised them from the time they were little puffs of fluff. She's always been nuts about poultry and as she's gotten older, she's really gotten...obsessed?" He smiled again. "I mean that in a nice way, of course." Lex's heart melted a little as he spoke. He really was a good guy.

"It's nice that she's able to move to a place where she can keep them."

"It was actually a challenge finding a place with enough of a yard to allow her ducks, but not too much to take care of. Another plus is that it's not that far from the clinic, so I can check on her easily. We only have to wait for the seller to finish vacating the premises." He started back toward his truck, and Lex fell into step. "Are you going to the Founder's Day picnic?" he asked as they walked.

"I hadn't planned on it." Danielle was busy, and she wasn't one to head to public events alone. Nope. She'd rather hole up in her basement and engrave silver. Or cut out copper cowboy boot Christmas decorations— her latest venture. Anything but be stared at as people speculated about her and Grady.

"I haven't been since visiting my grandparents as a kid, but I have good memories."

Lex tried to remember seeing Peter there at the celebration and couldn't do it.

"I was shy," Peter said, correctly guessing the direction of her thoughts. "And I usually stayed close to my grandparents, because they were nervous about me straying too far afield. But I had fun. Loved the fireworks and the games."

"I should have made more of an effort to get to know you," Lex said. "You only lived about a mile away." Which was close by rural standards.

"To tell you the truth," Peter said with a crooked smile, "you scared me."

"Really?" Huh. She'd never tried to be scary back then. Maybe it was simply part of her general personality.

"Well, you were cute and confident, and I was neither."

But he had been adorably awkward, and Lex had always liked him. She had no idea he'd been intimidated by her. Why couldn't Grady be intimidated by her?

"So, about that picnic?"

Lex gave him a frowning sidelong look.

Pete stopped next to his truck. "What I'm trying to do here is to ask you to go to Founder's Day with me. As a friend."

"Oh," Lex said on a note of surprise. "Well...yes. I'll do that."

"I've been so busy since moving home, starting a practice and helping my grandmother that I haven't had a chance to develop any kind of social network. I'd like to get out, but I don't want to go alone." He gave a self-conscious shrug. "To be honest, I did get invited to be a wingman for one of my associates, but I'm a rotten wingman. This will get me off the hook."

Lex laughed. "You know, a lot of time women prefer the wingman. You might want to rethink that."

"I'd rather go with you. Takes the pressure off."

"I'd love to go as a friend." Lex smiled easily, and Peter smiled back and she couldn't help wishing that she felt the same zing for him that she felt when Grady was near. Because if that happened, then she'd have an easier time convincing herself that she was simply reacting to a good-looking guy. Except that Peter was just as good-looking as Grady, and she was not reacting.

"Can I pick you up tomorrow at, say, three?"

"Three sounds great."

THE NEXT DAY Lex found herself looking forward to going to the Founder's Day Picnic with Peter. If she was going to be the object of gossip, why not spice things up by showing up with someone who wasn't Grady? The thought made her smile. Tiffani could take this and run with it.

She did her chores early, corralled everyone who needed corralling during her absence, then went in to shower. Afterward, she dried her hair and left it loose, slipped on a white eyelet sundress and cowboy boots, added a strand of turquoise and silver beads and a silver bracelet. Not bad.

And then the phone rang. Peter.

"I just got hit with a horse emergency. Barbed wire and a whole lot of stitches. If you still want to go, do you mind meeting me at the park?"

"Not at all."

"I understand if you'd rather not—"

"Peter. I'm happy to meet you there."

"Great. I'll keep you posted," he said, a smile in his voice. "And hopefully see you relatively soon."

"Good luck with the horse."

Feeling a twinge of disappointment, since she honestly did not want to attend the picnic alone, Lex opened the cupboard where the keys hung. After a moment's hesitation, she plucked off the key to her father's restored '56 GMC truck, which she'd started driving a few months before. Another small step in the healing process, and one that made her feel closer to her dad. They'd had such great times in the truck and when she was behind the wheel, she had a sense of him being there with her rather than a sense of loss. One small step forward.

When she got to the park, a van pulled out of a space near the rear of the packed parking lot, and Lex pulled in, hoping it was a sign that, despite her date being waylaid, it would be a good afternoon. She walked into the park as the line for barbecue was forming and Lissa Scott, Peter's vet tech, waved at her from a picnic table a few yards away.

"Peter told me to be on the lookout for you," she said as Lex approached. "He's not certain how long this will take, and he didn't want you to have to sit alone."

"That's really nice." Lex wasn't used to people doing things like that for her. Lissa patted the seat beside her and smiled. She was short and curvaceous and totally comfortable in her skin, which made Lex feel comfortable, too.

"I thought we'd sit a bit and wait for the line to shorten, unless you want to—"

"Not at all," Lex said. "So, did you know Peter back in the day?"

"I did not," she said. "Being a townie and not a rural kid." She tilted her head. "I really wanted to be a rural kid. I wanted horses and dogs and cats and pigs and chickens." She laughed. "What I got was a gerbil. Not that I didn't love Mr. Bill," she added hastily. "I did. But he wasn't the same as a dog."

The table shook then as two large bodies settled on

the opposite side, both carrying heaping plates of barbecue beef, potato salad, corn bread and green salad.

Well, dang.

"It's good to see you, Alexa." Todd flashed a smile at her before taking a long drink of beer.

"Likewise," she said coolly. So much for the parking spot being a harbinger of good fortune.

"Hey," Todd said, "let me introduce Brandon Ledford. Old college roomie here for the festivities. Brandon, this is Lissa and Lex."

"Nice to meet you," Lex and Lissa said almost simultaneously, Lissa sounding pleased and Lex sounding stony.

"Glad we could find two good-looking women to share our meal with," Brandon said.

"Except that we don't have meals," Lex pointed out.

"We're going to take care of that now," Lissa added. "See you soon."

"Not," she breathed as they got up from the table and headed for the line.

"Hurry back," Brandon called.

"Two of a kind," Lissa muttered. "I dated Todd once."

"I didn't. He thinks I missed out."

"You didn't. Pushy with a capital *P*. He thinks that his money and killer looks give him some kind of special rights." Lissa shot a look over her shoulder at the table they'd just vacated and then let out a small breath. "We're in luck. The table just filled up."

"Excellent," Lex said as they approached the line. "Should we hang back and wait for Peter?" She'd hoped he'd get there before they hit the serving area.

"He told me he wanted us to eat."

"Then I guess we'll eat." Kristen and Katie raced by with a pack of kids, and Lex smiled and waved then slowly lowered her hand as she caught sight of Grady standing near the outdoor bar with Jess and Ty Hayward, a beer in his hand. The bull riders had attracted several college-age women, and one of them intercepted Lex's gaze. The girl lifted her chin in a smug your-loss, my-gain look before turning back to Grady and the Hayward twins and taking hold of Grady's arm. Lex let out a small breath. As if she cared.

After she and Lissa had loaded their plates with beef, salad and corn on the cob, Lex purposely chose a table far from Todd and sat on the side that put her back to the bar so she didn't have to watch the women fawn over Grady and the Hayward twins. The table soon filled, and Lex found herself relaxing and talking to people she hadn't spoken to in ages.

"It's good to see you out and about," Lex's former English teacher said, and she realized that perhaps she had spent too much time in hermit mode. It had started when her father had died and somewhere along the line had become a habit. She ate slowly, enjoying the conversation and the company. Peter called as she finished her last bite of cherry cobbler.

"This is ugly," he said. "I may not make it."

Lex assured him she understood. "I'm having a great time with Lissa and will probably go home soon."

"Maybe we can make next year's picnic," Peter said with clear disappointment.

"I'll put it on my calendar," she said before wishing him luck and hanging up.

It hadn't been a bad afternoon at all, but she was ready to go. If Peter wasn't going to show, then she had no reason to stay. She'd made her appearance, and frankly it was tiring keeping an eye on Grady's whereabouts, which she felt she needed to do so that they didn't bump into each other. She wasn't in the bumping mood. Lissa had several friends sitting at the table with them, so Lex didn't feel bad leaning toward her and telling her she was going to take off a little early.

"If you're certain?" Lissa said.

"I am, but I have to say, you were a great date."

Lissa laughed. "Glad to accommodate."

And Lex was glad to leave. She'd had fun, but she was tired of being on guard. Public events always exhausted her. She tossed her plastic beer glass in the trash and was almost to her truck at the rear of the lot when someone called her name from behind. She turned to see Todd Lundgren sauntering toward her from the direction of the portable restrooms.

"You never rejoined us," he said as he came to a stop a few feet in front of her. One whiff of his breath confirmed what she'd suspected from his rolling gait. Todd had been drinking. A lot.

"Your table was full," she said.

"And now you're leaving?"

Duh.

"My date got waylaid."

He settled his hands on his oversize rodeo buckle— a buckle he most certainly didn't win. "So what if your date didn't show? That doesn't mean *you* have to leave."

"Excuse me," Lex said as she attempted to move past him. He stepped directly into her path, and she stopped, glaring up him. *Really?* Lex wasn't afraid of him, but she wasn't about to hang around and see what happened next.

"Think how much fun you could have if you stayed," he said, rocking back on his heels.

"Not interested."

"Ri-ight," he said in an exaggerated tone.

"Get over yourself, Todd, and get out of my way."

Anger flashed in his eyes. "Get over myself? Maybe you need to get over yourself."

Lex was about to tell him off when he reached out and took hold of the fob hanging out of her jacket pocket and plucked out her keys. Lex made a grab for them as they went by and missed.

"Really?" she asked, folding her arms over her chest, telling herself not to panic. It wasn't as though he was going to drive away in her father's truck. She hoped. But they weren't exactly in a place where people could easily see what was happening between them.

"Yeah," he said as he held the keys loosely in one hand. "Really."

She held out her hand. "I'm done playing. Give me the keys."

"Kiss me and I'll think about it."

Chapter Eleven

"Are you listening to me?" The girl named Sue gave Grady's arm a playful swat as she spoke.

No, he wasn't. He was watching Lex trying to talk Todd Lundgren into something. He could just see them at the edge of the parking lot if he craned his neck. Lex said something, and Todd smirked down at her and shook his head. She held out her hand, and he shook his head again.

She was trying to talk him out of his car keys.

Or if she wasn't, then she should have been, because the guy was hammered. Instead of walking away, she looked as if she was about to wrestle him for them, and somehow the thought of a drunken Todd Lundgren touching Lex was more than he could handle at the moment.

He smiled tightly at Sue, who was looking none too happy with him. "Excuse me."

He was already a few steps away before he heard her give a small snort and say, "Yeah. Sure."

It only took a matter of seconds for him to work his way through the cars to the rear of the lot, and as he approached, he heard Lex say, "I'm not kissing you. Give me the keys."

Grady felt his blood pressure spike. "Give her the keys," he said from a few yards away, jerking his head toward Lex as he continued to approach them.

"What keys?" Todd asked, his eyes narrowing.

"We can do this nice, or we can do this not so nice. Now give Lex the keys." And if she thought she was driving this guy home…well, then Grady was coming with them.

"This is between Lex and me," Todd insisted.

Grady looked directly at Lex then. "Do you want the keys?"

"Very much so."

Grady turned back to Todd, held out his hand then jerked it back when Todd spat. Shaking his head, he looked over his shoulder at Lex. "Call the sheriff. Public drunkenness."

A surprised look crossed her face, and then she pulled out her phone and started looking for the number while Grady stood chest to chest with Todd. When she punched in the last number, Todd dug into his pocket and with a muttered curse slammed the keys onto the ground at Lex's feet.

A single ugly word escaped his lips as he turned to go, and Grady grabbed him by the shoulder, itching to plant a fist in the guy's arrogant face. The only thing that stopped him was Lex's stony "Don't."

He gritted his teeth and released Todd, who stumbled a few steps, then headed off toward his friends standing near the food table.

Lex had the keys in her hand by the time Grady turned to face her. "I take it you weren't trying to drive him home?"

"He had *my* keys."

He almost asked why, then decided he didn't need to know. "Be more careful who you give your keys to."

"I didn't give them to him."

"He took them?" Grady shot another look at Todd's retreating back, thinking once again about what he might have to do to the guy.

"I need to go. Thank you."

He turned back to Lex. She seemed fine. Very… composed. He wondered. "You going to be okay?"

"I'm fine. I just need to get out of here."

Even though everything in him demanded that he see her home, make certain that she really was okay, he forced himself to nod. "If you need anything…"

"Yeah." She put the key in the truck door lock and twisted.

"Lex?"

"I said yes. I'll let you know if I need any help."

But she wouldn't. And they both knew that.

LEX DID NOT have an easy night.

How easy could it be when she forced herself to be honest and admit how glad she'd been to see Grady? Even though she'd been in a public place and could have started yelling for help if Todd had gotten too aggressive or tried something stupid, such as taking her father's truck, she'd been damned happy not to have had to do that.

So, yes. She'd been happy to see Grady, who'd quietly helped her out. No points gained or lost, no sense of him challenging her. Not his usual modus operandi, and she was half wondering what to make of his behavior. Something had shifted there. Because of their talk? Had Grady ever changed his behavior after one of their talks? Not that she could recall.

And she'd made such a huge point of saying she was never going to need him. And then she did. He hadn't mentioned it; hadn't taken the opportunity to rub it in.

It made her a touch uneasy, especially in light of the fact that he'd asked her out when she dropped off the twins' cough medication and ogled his naked chest and torso. His very muscular naked chest and torso with all those scars.

Scars that bothered her...but she didn't want to think about that, either.

So she did her best to shove Grady out of her head as she went about her morning chores, feeding Felicity and the dogs before heading out to fill the rest of the feeders and troughs. Ginger and Pepper dived into their dishes as usual, but Dave the Terror didn't bother getting up.

"Are you feeling all right?" Lex asked the terrier as she knelt by his bed. His nose was damp and cold. His gums had good color. He didn't seem to hurt anywhere, even if his stomach did seem a touch swollen.

She'd keep an eye on him and call Peter if the dog didn't perk up soon. Leaving the screen door propped open so the dogs could follow her when they'd finished eating, she made her way to the gate, then stopped dead in her tracks when she realized that the duck pen was empty.

Lex shot across the driveway and skidded to a stop next to the wire panels. And then she spotted the hole under the fence in the far corner and realized that the feed trough, which was never totally empty, looked as if it had been licked clean.

Dave.

Lex pressed her hand to her forehead and quickly started scouting the vicinity. Could these ducks fly? If so, where would they fly to?

Water.

There was only one body of water nearby—Fife's stock pond in the field adjoining hers. Lex started jogging across the pasture until she could see the pond and sure enough, there were ducks happily paddling about, oblivious of the fact that there were several good-size birds of prey circling the skies in nearby fields.

Ducks that she had to somehow catch.

Nancy would die if something happened to the little feathery beasts.

Lex started jogging back toward the house, wondering if her dad's fishing net was big enough for the job and how she was going to scoop a duck out of a half-acre pond. She was almost to the barn when she saw the truck parked next to hers.

Grady's truck.

Her heart skipped at the sight of him coming around the barn, but she'd deal with him later.

Whatever it was he'd been going to say died on his lips as he caught sight of her expression.

"I've got to catch some ducks," she said, opening the tack shed door and disappearing inside for long enough to rummage through her father's fishing equipment. When she found the net, she turned to see Grady standing in the doorway.

"Why do you have to catch ducks?"

"My dog tunneled into the pen and let them out." She brushed by him. "I think I need a gunnysack."

Grady reached out and took hold of her arm, stopping her in her tracks. "Lex. Slow down. I'm here to help."

She pulled in a breath. "Right."

"Show me what you're dealing with. Then we can get what we need."

She nodded and then started through the gate, half-afraid that the ducks, now that they'd tasted freedom, would take to the skies. Grady followed her to the pond, and they stood side by side on the bank, studying the ducks as they cheerfully chortled and swam.

"These ducks belong to a little old lady. They mean the world to her, and I am not going to have them end up being coyote or eagle dinner. Not on my watch."

Grady shot her a look. "What do these guys eat?"

"Pond stuff," she said, pointing to the duck that had just disappeared under the water and then come up gobbling down green goop that would surely have horrified Nancy.

"There has to be some kind of ducky aphrodisiac that will bring them back to shore."

"I have duck treats, but I'm sure they're not as good as pond scum."

He pulled out his phone. "Duck treats," he muttered as he typed. "Cucumber, lettuce, watermelon, bananas, grapes, vegetables…" He looked up. "Do you have any of those?"

"Watermelon. Frozen peas." She hadn't been shopping in a while.

"Do you want to stay here and ward off the coyotes and eagles or get the watermelon?"

"I'll get the melon," she said with a quirk of her lips. She hesitated, then said, "Thanks."

"We haven't caught them yet." His expression was serious. There was no edge of amusement or sense that he was going to use this to his advantage later.

"I mean thanks for not leaving. After...everything."

The look he gave her made her stomach drop a little and blood rush to her cheeks. "No problem."

Why did she feel this stupid bond with him, and so certain that now that he was here, everything would be okay? Since when did she need anyone to handle anything? She turned and headed back to the house, feeling as if she were escaping. Well, if she was, she was soon heading back to whatever she'd escaped from, carrying chopped-up watermelon in a bowl.

Lex had expected more traumas, perhaps a dunking in the pond, but catching the ducks turned out to be ridiculously easy. She tossed a juicy chunk of watermelon into the water, and Channing instantly gobbled it up as his ladies swam closer to investigate the interesting splash. Grady reached into the bowl and tossed the next chunk closer to shore. Channing took the bait.

After that it was simply a matter of making a watermelon trail leading toward the pen. Once the final duck was out of the water, Lex fell in behind and helped herd them back to captivity. Grady plugged the hole with a big rock when they were back in their pen, and then the ducks were once again in stir, happily eating the rest of the melon.

"Are your dogs electric fence savvy?" Grady asked, tipping his ball cap back as he studied the pen.

"I have one around the garden to keep the rabbits out."

"What do you say we put it around the duck pen? It'll also deter hungry coyotes."

"Excellent plan. I could do it myself."

"Because you don't like help?" Again that almost too-serious gaze.

She cocked her head. "Actually…no." More words piled into her head, but she ignored them. Went with the simple truth. "More like I don't want to trouble you."

And she did not want him to leave. She didn't yet know what she wanted, but she was done being rude to Grady and tired of battling this attraction. The attraction was real and this new Grady—the one who quietly helped her without mocking or taunting—was upsetting her equilibrium. Making her uncertain of what she did or didn't want. If she let her brain run the show, she'd probably have sent him on his way after thanking him profusely for helping with the ducks. If her feelings were running the show, she would have kissed him when she'd thanked him. She'd done neither…and that meant?

Hell, she didn't know.

She cleared her throat and continued. "I appreciated your help last night, and I also appreciated the fact that you didn't take the opportunity to rub it into my face…you know…after I made such a big deal about not needing anyone."

"I wouldn't have done that," he said. "Not in that type of situation. How'd he get your keys, anyway?"

"Just reached out and took them."

"I felt like reaching out and belting him."

"Me, too. But he kind of scared me." She'd told herself he didn't scare her while she'd been facing off with him, but after he left, she'd felt an insane rush of relief.

An odd expression crossed Grady's face. "Glad I was there. Now let's see about this fence."

"That would be nice." Why did her voice sound so stiff all of a sudden? "Maybe I could cook you a steak or something. As a thank-you."

"I wouldn't say no to that." And suddenly he seemed as self-conscious as she was. "Maybe I could transfer the fence while you deal with the steak? Save some time."

"Yeah. That would work."

She walked with him to the garden where the low-powered solar electric fence kept her lettuce and spinach safe. There was only enough charge to startle, but she figured it would keep Dave from digging more holes to get at the duck food and also keep wild animals out. She should have thought of this sooner, but she'd expected the dogs to keep the wildlife away, not to let the ducks out.

Once Grady was busy pulling fence stakes, she went into the house and looked into the freezer. A steak was a good idea, except that she didn't have one. Dang. She really needed to stock up more often.

She leaned back against the counter and squeezed her forehead with her palm. Her life had been so much easier before Grady came back to help his sister. So. Much. Easier.

A few seconds later she was back in at the garden. "I don't have a steak."

He looked up at her, then continued rolling the white electrical strapping. "Let me get this done and we'll make a plan."

"All right," she said instead of arguing. She was tired of arguing. Instead she wanted to stand and watch

Grady work, admire the muscles rippling beneath his T-shirt, watch his profile as he concentrated on what he was doing. He looked up and caught her midstare. She didn't look away. Didn't even consider it.

"Lex?"

"Yes?"

"Stop looking at me like that."

Lex's heart rate bumped up, but she didn't shift her gaze. "Or what?" she asked softly, warmth flooding through her as he sent her a scorching look in return.

"Or I'll have to do something about it."

"Yeah?"

He frowned, gave her a few seconds to change her mind, then carefully set down the strapping on the ground. Lex stood planted where she was, her heart thumping against her ribs as he closed the distance between them in a few strides. Once in front of her, he took her face in his hands, the calluses on his palms rough against her skin. He wasn't that much taller than her, so it was easy to meet his mouth as it came down, easy to shove her hands into his hair, knocking his hat off. Easy to work her lips across the stubbled planes of his cheeks to nuzzle his ear, nip his earlobe, then bring her mouth back to his to be consumed.

Her body was on fire with need, and she realized that if Grady really wanted to do a number on her, he'd walk away right now. Just rip himself away from her, get into his truck and leave, because if he did, she didn't know if she would ever recover. She needed him. Grady. Needed him. Now.

He once again took her face between his rough palms, bringing his forehead down to touch hers. "What are we going to do, Lex?"

"We're going into my house," she said, her voice husky and low.

"You're certain, because if you're not—"

She cut his words off with a kiss and once it ended, he took her by the hand and they headed through the garden, up the path to her house. They stopped at the door for another long kiss, and that was when Lex realized that her hands were shaking. Had she ever wanted anyone so badly that her hands had shaken? No.

They stumbled into the house, still kissing, and then Lex led him down the hall to her bedroom, to the place where, if she was honest with herself, she'd known for some time they'd end up. She'd been trying for the past several weeks to get Grady out of her system and failed miserably. The only other option was complete immersion. She was going to experience Grady, and that, she figured, would either cure her or drag her down deeper. She was willing to take the chance.

Once they were in the bedroom and the door had been closed against the dogs, he stepped back, as if giving her one more chance to say no. She reached up and took hold of the snaps on her shirt, popping the first three in quick succession. His hands came up to cover hers; then he continued what she had started, slowly unsnapping. When the last snap was free, he pushed open her shirt, his fingers brushing against her skin. She shivered but not from any kind of cold.

"Lace," he muttered. Lex frowned at him and he said, "Never mind."

Never mind indeed, when his mouth was on her breasts, first through her bra, making her crazy, then on her skin as he pushed the lace aside and continued his exploration. Lex's head dropped back, and then when she didn't think she could take any more, she lifted his head with both hands, tilting it up.

"Out of 'em," she said, pointing at his boots.

Grady complied, as did she; jeans quickly followed, and then anything else that got between herself and total Grady immersion.

His body was even harder than she'd imagined, all lean muscle and sinew. And scars. So many scars, some simple white marks, others raised flesh beneath her fingers. She closed her eyes against them and simply let her fingers explore. Never had she touched a guy like this, and she found she didn't want to stop.

She didn't—not until Grady rolled on top of her, positioning himself to claim her.

"Nightstand," she said, her hands running lightly over his side as he reached over her to open the drawer, found her one and only condom, tore it open and rolled it on.

Her breath caught as he slowly pushed into her, inch by glorious inch, watching her reaction. No. Savoring her reaction. He was all about making her feel good, and what she'd assumed would be a quick ride turned out to be a long, slow marathon in which he brought her close so many times that she was almost whimpering by the time he brought her over the edge. Grady soon followed, and she clung to him until his body stilled. Then she buried her face into the hollow of his neck, inhaling deeply. He smelled so damned good.

A few seconds later he rolled onto his back, pulling her with him. Lex stretched out along his side, resting her head on his chest and feeling his heart beat beneath her cheek.

Grady brought his hand up to stroke her hair. "Hope nothing got to the ducks while we were busy."

Laughter bubbled up Lex's throat, taking away all sense of postcoital awkwardness. She glanced up at him, and he smiled down at her. A tired, satisfied, found-what-I-wanted smile that for some reason didn't frighten her as much as it should have. Not right then, anyway, because she found that denial worked two ways. She could also deny that real life was going to come crashing in on them as soon as they got out of bed. At this point in time, it was only her and Grady and the quiet of her bedroom, the feel of his damp skin below her cheek, his hand stroking through her hair.

His fingers dropped lower to move over her arm in a light caress. "Any chance we might do this again?"

Lex exhaled, her breath fanning over his chest, and she felt him still as he waited for her answer. "I'd be lying if I said no."

His arm tightened around her. "You just made me a very happy man."

Chapter Twelve

And so it went. For the next two weeks, Grady happened by Lex's place in the early evenings after Annie was home and the girls were fed. Sometimes they talked, sometimes he lent her a hand around the place but they always ended up making love.

Despite her toughness and willingness to take on the world, Lex had insecurities, which she did her best to hide—even from him. Her lover.

That was what Grady planned to work on during the time they had together before he had to hit the road again…getting Lex to open up to him. Helping her see that he was an ally, not someone to defend against or hold things from. He was making some headway, slowly but surely. He got her to admit that, yes, she'd thought he was hot even when she was eviscerating him earlier that summer. No, she hadn't thought he was hot when he was dating Danielle—well, maybe a little, but she'd been really worried about her friend.

"You had cause," he admitted as he held her for a few minutes before he had to roll out of bed and put on his boots and jeans and head back to his sister's place. Annie wouldn't have cared if he spent the night somewhere, but she assumed he was at Hennessey's and he didn't dissuade her. Lex wasn't ready for people to know about them.

The rampant rumors that had been bandied about before they actually started sleeping together had cooled down, and when they were together in public, they made it a point to be civil and friendly. No sparks. They sat together during lessons, close, but not too close. Lex made it a point to chat with the parents, and he made it a point not to hang with her when she did that. They looked like friends. Or casual acquaintances. And he was good with that if it made Lex feel better about the situation.

For now.

"You and Danielle truly are polar opposites," Lex said musingly. "Strange that you even got together in the first place."

"No—that's why we got together. That opposites-attract thing. For what it's worth, I truly thought I loved her."

"I know."

"But—" he ran a caressing hand over her back "—I didn't work too hard to preserve our relationship when the hard times came. When I had to choose." He brought his hand up to tangle in her silky hair. "But then…neither did she."

He could tell that Lex hadn't thought about that angle of his breakup with her best friend—that despite being upset, Danielle hadn't exactly chased him down to patch things up. "This guy she's with now? Do you think it's a good relationship?"

"I do. I think they're very well suited." Lex traced a pattern on his abdomen, following a scar. He'd had to explain to her that not all of his scars were from bull riding or from surgery following bull riding. Some of the ones on his torso and a few on his arms and legs were from when he'd had a nasty encounter with a car while riding his bike as a kid.

She'd seemed oddly relieved, but he couldn't believe the scars really mattered to her, other than giving her trails to trace on his body, which he kind of loved. If anyone understood bull riding, it was Lex, and he was glad of that. It gave them a chance, and he realized as the days passed, he really wanted a chance with her. He'd never felt so at peace with a woman, which was something, since Lex didn't inspire visions of tranquility.

"I need to get back," he said, reluctantly pushing up to a sitting position. Lex sat, too, the sheets pooling at her waist, making him want to make love to her all over again. He could not get enough of her, and from the smile playing across her face as she watched him get out of bed, the feeling was mutual.

He and Lex.

Go figure.

But the bond was there. A strong one. Stronger than anything he'd experienced with a woman. It was more than physical attraction, more than being a friend. She challenged him yet accepted him. She made him want to be a better man.

When he got home that night a little after dark, Annie was sitting on the porch. The sounds of the television filtered through the open window at the opposite end from where she sat, a tall glass of iced tea in her hand. Grady crossed the porch and took the chair next to her.

"There's tea in the fridge."

"I'm good." And he was.

"You haven't been to Hennessey's lately," Annie said casually.

"Nope." Busted.

"A customer mentioned she hadn't seen you lately, and since her son practices pretty frequently there…"

Grady spread his fingers on the wicker chair arms. "I've been going to Lex's place. Helping her out."

A small smile played on his sister's face, the kind she used to have just before she leveled him with some zinger when they were kids. "That's nice of you."

"Yeah. She has these ducks that she's keeping. They needed their fence reinforced."

"And everyone knows that Lex is all thumbs and couldn't possibly do something like that for herself."

He smiled a little. "She likes the company."

"As I thought."

His expression grew serious. He wasn't surprised that Annie had caught on, but he didn't want to upset Lex. "People don't know. Lex wants to keep things quiet for now."

"Obviously, since *I* didn't know." But she was still smiling as she fixed her gaze on the garage that he'd finished siding several days ago. Once he finished the shed, he was free to hit the road and maybe a rodeo or two before he started competing in the Bull Extravaganza. He wasn't yet ready to go.

"I'm thinking of asking her to go to the rodeo with me and the girls."

"Nice idea."

"You don't mind?"

She turned her head toward him. "If you take the

girls to the rodeo, it might be good for you to have some backup."

"I take them to riding lessons every week without backup."

"Just saying that the rodeo might be different." She took a sip of tea. "The girls have told me that you spend all your time sitting with Lex at lessons. You shouldn't fool yourself into thinking that no one is aware."

"Good to know."

"What's the big secret, anyway?"

"I'm letting Lex take the lead here. I think this thing, me and her, kind of blindsided her."

"I don't think so."

Grady looked at her, surprised. Annie gave him a pitying look. "When you two were around each other earlier this month, I'm surprised smoke wasn't rolling off your backs. I think she was aware."

"Smoke. Really." Annie nodded at him. "Huh." He glanced back up at the sky. Stars were starting to show from between the clouds.

"When you told me you liked her a few weeks ago…I have to admit that I didn't think you had a chance. I felt sorry for you because Lex can be—"

"Formidable?"

"Yes. Accurate description." She laughed and reached out to give his shoulder a sisterly squeeze. "I'm glad for the two of you. Who knows, maybe now you'll have a reason to stay."

He smiled back at her. "No matter what, I have a reason to stay."

Annie kept looking at her funny.

Or maybe it was that she wasn't really looking at

her, as if she was afraid that if she did she might smile or something.

She knew.

Lex reached across the antique table for another stack of tulle circles. She counted out eight Jordan almonds, set them in the center of the top circle, brought the edges together to make a bundle and then tied it with pale blue ribbon and tossed it into a half-full basket. Wedding crafts were tedious work, but until today she'd rather enjoyed the half an hour she and Danielle and Annie spent during their lunch hour making favors during the past week.

Had Grady spilled the beans?

If so, that was fine. Even if she was still self-conscious about people knowing her business.

Annie met her eyes, and this time she did smile. A nice smile, not a catty one, and Lex exhaled. Forced herself to relax—as much as that were possible.

The bell rang over the door and Annie excused herself to see to the customer.

"Just tell her that you know that she knows that you're sleeping with Grady."

Lex's gaze snapped up to Danielle's. "Is this common knowledge?" she finally asked.

"A common guess. Both you and Grady have been in excellent spirits, and he hasn't been to Hennessey's much over the past two weeks." She wrapped a ribbon around a tulle bundle. "And you haven't said one negative thing about him lately."

"Okay…" she said, dropping her eyes to the almonds she was counting out.

"It's a good thing," Danielle said.

"You think so?"

Danielle flashed that beautiful smile of hers. "Of course. You and Grady are so much better suited to each other than he and I ever were. I think with us, it was the novelty of being together. I mean…it might have worked out, but—" she wiggled the finger with her engagement ring "—I'm glad it didn't."

Annie came back through the beaded curtains. "Tiffani Crenshaw looking for a statement ring." She met Lex's gaze. "I told you she'd be back."

"You should probably send her flowers," Danielle said mildly, thus setting the stage for Lex to confess if she cared to.

Lex let out a breath. She needed to get over this rampant need for privacy in all things…well…private. She tied a ribbon around tulle, tightening it, then said to Annie, "Grady and I are seeing each other."

Annie's face broke into a wide smile. "I know," she said happily.

Lex stared at her. "Apparently everybody *knows*," she muttered, mimicking Annie's tone, but not in a malicious way. "It may not last."

"There are no guarantees," Annie agreed. "Just… enjoy each other while you can."

Lex's gaze shifted from Danielle to Annie, then back to Danielle. A moment later a genuine smile broke free, and she leaned back in her chair, putting the palms of both hands on the table in front of her. It felt good to no longer be harboring a secret from those she was closest to. Or to believe she was harboring a secret.

"That's good advice. Thank you."

Lex spent the next two evenings alone. Grady had to get in some practice bull rides, and frankly she'd be worried about him if he didn't. He needed to stay on top of his game. End of story.

She wouldn't allow herself to think of anything beyond that; she wasn't going to dwell on how he got the scars that weren't caused by the car-meets-boy-on-bike incident when he was eleven. She wasn't going to remember every bad thing she'd ever seen happen in the bull-riding arena. No. She would focus on the here and now, because that was what they had. The present.

Besides that, if anyone was prepared to handle bull riding, it was her. So what if she'd almost puked the one time she went to Hennessey's to teach Grady a lesson? It was her first time near an arena since her father died. It was to be expected.

She went to bed early the second night, but just after she'd turned the porch lights off, she heard Grady's truck pull in and met him at the door. He took her face between his hands as he always did when he kissed her the first time. She could smell the arena dust on him and it made her heart rise in her throat.

"I'm only here for a minute. Regretfully. One of the twins is sick, and I'm sure the other is about to go down. They're both cranky."

"I can imagine."

"But…" He smiled down at her. "I have tickets for the rodeo in Bozeman next weekend, and I'm going to take the girls if they're well enough. Want to come along?"

There was no reason for her to say *no*, not now that everyone was aware of their relationship, but she could see from his expression that Grady half expected her to say *no*. Did he think she might be afraid?

"All right." She heard the words come out of her

mouth, wondered if she'd said them because she actually wanted to go or to prove that she wasn't afraid.

"We, uh, don't have to stay for the bulls. You know…if that would be difficult."

"I'm good."

"Are you sure?" He held her loosely by the shoulders, his forehead coming close to hers as he said, "Because I totally understand if—"

"Either you want me to go to the rodeo or you don't."

Grady's eyebrows pulled together. "I want you to go," he said quietly.

"As do I." She attempted a casual smile, suspected it came off as brittle and forced, but it would have to do. She had nothing more to offer at the moment.

"I might not see you between now and then," Grady said. "I'm rustier than I thought and have to put in the practice time. And help out with the girls until they feel better."

"I understand." She was startled to hear her voice become husky as she spoke, to sound as if it was on the edge of cracking, and because of that, when she kissed him goodbye a few minutes later, she held back a little. She had her faults, but being needy wasn't one of them. Grady needed to understand that.

After he left, walking down the path to his truck, his shoulders held more stiffly than usual, a wave of anxiety crashed over her, taking her breath, making her knees feel suddenly weak.

Lex pressed her hand to her chest and inhaled deeply as her heart clutched. What was going on? Was this an anxiety attack?

She had no other name to put on it.

Okay, maybe one visit to Hennessey's arena hadn't

been enough to lay all ghosts to rest. Maybe the thought of going to a rodeo bothered her more than she'd acknowledged, but she could do this. It wasn't as if she was afraid of bull riding, because it hadn't been a bull that had taken her father out. It'd been a weak vessel in his heart, not a horn or a hoof.

She needed to get a grip.

When Grady's headlights came on, cutting across her yard and reflecting off the barn, Lex turned away from the window and walked through her house to the kitchen, stepping over sleeping dogs on the way. She poured a glass of water, took a long drink and told herself she felt better.

Her biggest fear in going to the rodeo was probably that of crying in front of the kids. Seeing an actual bull-riding event would remind her of the fact that her father would never set foot in an arena again. That was going to be tough to deal with—but not something she couldn't manage. She'd been fine.

PETE'S GRANDMOTHER CAME with him to transport her beloved ducks to their new home, and the cute thing was that she seemed to be more excited by their new quarters than her own.

"You should see the yard," Nancy said as she held Channing in her arms, stroking the top of his head. Lex wasn't certain if she was talking to her or the drake but took a chance and said, "I'm sure it's lovely."

"You will come by and visit, won't you?"

"Most assuredly."

"Maybe we could have a barbecue or something," Peter said. "Invite your friends."

"That would be lovely," Nancy said with a broad smile. "You'll come, won't you, Alexa?"

"Certainly." Although she was getting the feeling that Nancy had more in mind than a backyard barbecue for her and Pete. Pete also seemed to get his grandmother's meaning. He met Lex's gaze over Nancy's head and lifted his eyebrows in a way that clearly conveyed that he was humoring her.

"She's been trying to set me up with every single female in the vicinity," Pete said as Lex helped him load the duck pen panels. "It's getting hard to take her to the grocery store because most of the checkers are single, and you should see what Lissa has to put up with."

Lex bit her lip so that she didn't smile. "Probably wants great-grandchildren."

"Do not think that subject hasn't arisen," Pete muttered, hefting the empty pond in the back of the truck. They both turned toward Nancy, who stood several yards away, still holding Channing. She beamed at them, and they turned back to the truck at the same time.

"Yes. Good luck with that," Lex murmured.

"If you do come to the barbecue, bring Grady. That'll get you out of the line of fire."

"Uh…yeah. I'll do that." Although she didn't know how long Grady would be in the area. He'd be leaving soon, but they hadn't spoken about when. Or his coming back. In fact, they hadn't spoken at all since he invited her to the rodeo, three nights ago. And she was good with that. Or so she told herself.

After Peter and Nancy drove away, Lex walked to where the pen had stood. Dave the Terror sniffed around the area while Lex gathered up the electric fencing that she and Grady had installed after the first time they made love.

She carried it to the storage shed, since the rabbits had already had their way with the garden during its absence, feeling sad as she dumped the stakes and strapping into a corner. It was a fine thing when an electric fence brought forth sentimental feelings.

Was she losing control here?

No. Because she didn't lose control. And what was with the sadness? She had nothing to feel sad about.

Except that she did miss Grady.

GRADY STAYED AT Hennessey's for longer than he'd intended, helping a couple of high school kids, and then he went out for a beer with the Hayward twins. It was dark by the time he headed for home, but he turned down Lex's road anyway. He needed to see her, and if her lights were on, he was stopping.

The only room lit when he drove into her driveway was her bedroom, and he told himself that counted, even though it was late. But another light came on as he neared her front walk where he usually parked, and she was on the porch by the time he got out of his truck.

She didn't say a word as he came up the steps. Instead she met him halfway across the porch, walked into his embrace, wrapping her arms around his waist and pressing her cheek against his as he held her tightly against him. Raising his head, he smoothed her hair back from her face with both hands, then kissed her deeply.

Lex melted into him and then it was a matter of getting into the house, up the stairs to her room, shedding clothing as they went. He felt as if he hadn't seen her in weeks, not days, and as they fell into her bed, he was rocked by how very much he needed her. It was about so much more than sex. It was about…Lex. The way she made him feel, the way she challenged him and supported him and…completed him.

Yeah. His life felt different and more complete.

"I missed you," he said after they'd made love and were lying entwined on top of the quilts, because neither of them had had the patience to pull them off or fold them back. Four days without her had been four very long days. What was it going to be like when he was back on the road?

"I missed you, too," she murmured against his chest as she traced her favorite scar near his shoulder—the one from the bull in Dallas that'd managed to hook his upper arm, completely ruining his favorite shirt and necessitating sixteen stitches. There was a note in her voice, something approaching wonder.

Grady closed his eyes, inhaled the fragrance of her hair, tried not to think about why missing him would be such a wondrous thing. Maybe, like him, she was getting to the point where it was hard to imagine life alone. Their relationship had snowballed faster than he had expected, faster than he really knew how to deal with. So what he was doing was taking one day at a time, one small moment at a time. One challenge at a time.

The Bozeman Rodeo was his next challenge.

Lex fell silent after saying that she missed him, and they lay together, idly caressing and thinking deep thoughts. But Lex didn't push him away or withdraw, so when he finally got up to head home, Grady felt everything was okay between them. He wasn't fool enough to think that going to the rodeo was going to be easy for Lex, regardless of what she said, and he was no longer fool enough to ask her about it. Sore subject. So they would simply deal with it together when the time came. No sense fighting the battle early and sparking a few more along the way.

LEX WALKED GRADY to the door, kissed him good-night then leaned her head against the oak frame after closing the door. His boots echoed on her porch and then his truck started and still she stood, leaning her forehead against the aged wood.

She was scared and working so hard not to be.

She had missed him over the past four days. Missed him so much that when she'd heard his truck drive in, she practically raced down the stairs.

How was this a good thing? What was she setting herself up for?

Lex pushed off from the door and sat on her sofa, staring across the dimly lit room. She cared for Grady. If she didn't, she wouldn't be sleeping with him. But it was a temporary thing. They both knew that. He'd go back on the circuit. She'd stay here. Yes, he said he was wintering on his sister's property, but she'd believe that when she saw it. Oklahoma would call—better weather, more opportunities to practice.

A small part of her, though—the part that stirred up trouble and gave her anxiety attacks—whispered that if Grady said he was going to do something, he was going to do it. He wasn't leaving.

She pushed the thought down. Buried it as deeply as she could.

As much as she was enjoying their time together, it was transitory. It had to be. Grady was fun. He was a good friend. He was her lover for now. Not someone she'd lie awake nights worrying about because of what he did for a living.

Especially because of what he did for a living. She'd grown up in the business. How many bull riders did she know who'd had great careers and retired hale and hearty? Maybe a little creaky in the joints and scarred up, but alive and well? Lots. So it wasn't his career.

Much.

Those damned scars.

Lex got to her feet and stalked into the kitchen. She'd get a handle on this. Oh, yes, she would. And once he was on tour in the fall and not readily available, she'd develop a new perspective. One that wasn't colored by his proximity. A more realistic view of the situation.

And on that thought, Lex turned off the kitchen light and headed upstairs to the bed the man who was driving her crazy had so recently vacated. She pulled the quilts back and climbed under the sheet…then buried her head in the pillow and drew in Grady's scent.

Chapter Thirteen

The twins talked nonstop on the drive to the rodeo, and Lex was impressed by Grady's patience as he good-humoredly answered their many, many questions. She was feeling more positive about the trip, about Grady, about everything. After her late-night talk with herself, she'd fallen asleep and woken up feeling better. More centered. More in control. The feeling had continued for the entire day and when Grady had picked her up early this morning, she was certain that the anxiety she'd felt after he drove away two nights ago was caused solely by her repressed concern about watching a bull-riding event.

Which in turn convinced her that she needed to be more honest with herself.

After arriving, the twins wanted to do about fifty things—see the bucking horses, go to the carnival, eat everything that Annie had requested they not eat.

"Sometimes one must cave in the name of survival," Grady said as he handed each girl a caramel apple.

"Agreed," Lex said with a laugh.

Moments later they were helping the girls mop sticky goo off their chins and their new Western shirts.

"I think Annie knew what she was talking about," Lex murmured.

"Uncle Grady! I lost a tooth!" Kristen pulled a tiny white nugget out of her apple and held it up.

"Cool." He took the tooth, wrapped it in the tissue Lex automatically handed him and tucked it into his shirt pocket.

"Snap the flap," Kristen directed, pushing her tongue through the space where her tooth had been.

"Will do." He nodded at Katie. "Try to keep all your teeth, all right?"

Katie laughed and bit deeply into her apple, giving Lex the distinct impression that she was trying for all she was worth to lose one of her teeth.

"The line's getting long," Lex said. "Let's grab some seats."

They each took a twin by the hand and then, since they had nothing to do with their free hands, they joined them, walking to the ticket line with the bouncing girls. They were lucky enough to get seats under the awning so that they weren't baking in the sun and almost as soon as they were settled, the twins announced in unison that they had to use the bathroom.

"I'll take them," Lex said. "If you don't mind saving the seats."

Even though they protested, she talked the twins into taking off their pink cowboy hats and setting them on the seats they'd just vacated. "You do want to sit by Uncle Grady when we get back, right?"

"Yes," Kristen agreed.

"But we won't sit right next to him," Katie added. "'Cause that's where you're supposed to sit."

"Right." She'd tried to sit on the end, thus hemming the girls in, but they'd have none of that.

"Are you going to marry Uncle Grady?" Kristen piped up as Lex shrugged out of her jacket to leave it on her chair.

"I...uh..." She met Grady's gaze and found that she couldn't read his expression.

"That's not a question you ask people," he said to Kristen.

"Why not?"

"Because," he said with an easy smile, "that's something people tell you when they're ready and not before. So there's no sense asking early."

"Oh." Kristen gave a shrug. "Okay. But you'll tell us first?"

Grady smiled. "When we're ready."

And Lex found she couldn't meet his eyes after that. She edged past him; then when she reached the stairs, she took a twin's hand in each of hers and headed for what would no doubt be a wait for the restroom. Plenty of time to think and possibly fend off curious questions. But while the twins had plenty of commentary, they took Grady's words to heart and didn't ask anything about her and their uncle.

When they made it back to their seats again and settled, Grady put his arm around Lex. The girls exchanged glances, hunching their shoulders and smiling as if they were party to a glorious secret.

Lex sighed, and Grady's arm tightened around her. She gave up and leaned in to him, telling herself that in the name of honesty, she needed to admit that she liked being held by him.

"Sorry about that," he whispered into her ear, his

breath fanning over her cheek. She nodded without looking at him. It was no big deal, after all. Of course the twins thought in terms of marriage. That was how all their fairy tales and movies ended. The guy and girl get married and live happily ever after. She only hoped they weren't too disappointed if it didn't work out that way. The little girls had kind of wormed their way into Lex's heart.

She relaxed once the rodeo started, enjoying both the action in the arena and the twins' commentary. They had to go to the bathroom again during the second section of team roping, and then they tried to talk Grady into a hot dog but he told them they'd eat on the way home and they didn't want to spoil their appetite.

"I'm going to be a barrel racer," Katie announced, which pleased Lex no end—not because she wanted to run barrels, but because she was so much more confident about her horsemanship.

"Not me," Kristen said. "I'm gonna rope."

"Okay," Grady said to Lex. "I'll go home and tell Annie she needs to start saving for two thirty-thousand-dollar horses so that the girls can be competitive."

"I guess that's the beauty of rough stock," Lex agreed. "All you need is your saddle. Or rope."

"A decent set of spurs."

"Medical insurance." She felt herself sober after that. Grady touched her chin and when she turned her head, he kissed her lightly before taking her hand in his and setting it on his thigh.

"Don't get ticked with me for asking, but do you want to leave early? Before the bulls."

Lex swallowed. "I think I'll be okay."

"I'm right here."

Yes, he was. Right there. Propping her up, when Lex had been raised with the notion that people shouldn't need propping up, and that tore at her almost as much as the thought of watching the bullfighters.

But she was going to be strong for the girls. "I'll be all right."

And she was—to a degree. She tensed up when she heard the clangs of metal as the bulls were loaded into the chutes. Tensed up even more when the bullfighters came out and started doing their bit. One of them mugged for the crowd. The other stood quietly near the chutes, which was what her father had done. He wasn't there to entertain. He'd been there to save lives. And he did. A number of them.

Lex blinked a few times. Cleared her throat.

The announcer came on with a blare of music and announced that the final event would start in a matter of minutes. "And by the way, folks, I've just gotten word that we have a pretty danged famous bull rider here in the crowd. Local boy, too. Grady Owen! Give a wave! Let the people see you!"

Grady gamely raised his hand as people craned their necks to get a look at him.

"Heading off to New York City pretty soon, aren't you, son?" the announcer asked. "That's right, folks. Grady is going to represent us at the Bull Extravaganza. As you know, they only let the best of the best into that competition. Let's give old Grady a hand and wish him good luck."

The audience clapped, and the people sitting behind them reached forward to pat his shoulders. Grady's fingers tightened around Lex's, and she felt as if she were about to hyperventilate.

Why?

She was tougher than this. Why was everything getting to her all of a sudden?

"Let's go," Grady said.

"I—"

"There'll be more rodeos in the future." He got to his feet and Lex did the same, feeling like a loser, but also feeling the need to escape. It was hard to breathe and she felt light-headed.

"But—" Kristen caught the look Grady sent her and abruptly stopped speaking.

"We'll see the bulls at the next rodeo, pumpkin."

"All right." The disappointed words came out softly, breaking Lex's heart.

"I'm sorry about that," Lex said once they were in the truck. Grady looped an arm around her neck and kissed her. "I don't know what happened."

"It's okay," he said, putting the truck in gear. "Right, girls?"

"Right," they said unenthusiastically.

But it wasn't right. Lex knew it in her gut. Today had been a perfect storm of emotions, past and present, coming together to devastate her. She'd never once questioned the fact that Grady would resume his career. Had lain awake thinking about it, trying to contain her growing anxiety, convincing herself that it was natural to be concerned. Who wouldn't be? Grady was her friend. Her summer lover.

So why did she suddenly feel a hole opening up in her life? A hole that felt very much like the one she'd experienced when her dad died?

A hole that had taken her years to only partially fill. Did she want to go through that again? Keeping busy so that she wouldn't think? Filling her farm with animals that needed her?

She didn't have any more room on the farm, and to be honest, she didn't know if she had any more room in her heart. Not for someone who would leave another gaping chasm behind.

GRADY DIDN'T MAKE the mistake of trying to make small talk on the drive home. Lex was silently working through matters in her head, and if the frown knitting her brow was any indication, they were serious matters. Him-and-her matters.

By the time they dropped the twins off, his stomach was so tight it felt like a walnut.

"How was it?" Annie asked as she met the truck to help the twins out before Grady took Lex home.

"We didn't get to see the bulls," Katie said. "But Lex 'splained about that on the way home, so it's okay." Lex had told the girls that her dad used to be a bullfighter and now that he was gone, it was hard for her to see bullfighters. The girls had been both impressed and empathetic, and Lex's simple explanation had eased the tension on the drive home. The tension with the girls, anyway. There was still a lot unsaid between the two of them, and he had a feeling whatever was coming down the pike wasn't good.

"And I lost a tooth!" Kristen announced. Grady opened his pocket and passed the tissue-wrapped treasure to his sister through the window. Annie gave him a questioning look, and he responded with an imperceptible shake of his head.

"Okay, ladies. Into the house." The girls headed up the walk, Annie behind them. She turned and waved as

Grady put the truck in gear. The drive to Lex's house was silent. Fine, they'd talk when they got there… only they didn't. Lex was in serious self-defense mode.

"Maybe going to the rodeo wasn't such a great idea," he said, breaking the brittle silence after pulling the truck to a stop in front of her house.

"I have to face it sometime." She half turned toward him in the seat. "I know we have issues to discuss, but not now. Not tonight."

He didn't know if she wanted time to calm down or time to build up her defenses. Either way, there wasn't much he could do except to nod in agreement.

"We will talk," she promised as she reached for the door handle, as if she assumed he thought she might try to dodge the matter. He didn't.

"I know," he said in a stony voice. Lex got out of the truck and walked around the front. He waited until she unlocked her door and went inside, surrounded by bouncing, happy dogs; then once the lights came on he put his truck in gear.

Was this shades of the Danielle situation all over again? Would he have to choose between the woman he loved and bull riding?

If so, he knew in his gut that, difficult as it might be, he would choose differently than the way he did the last time.

Lex was getting tired of living in a state of anxiety, and now she knew why it was happening. She'd promised herself while grieving for her father that she would never, ever hurt like that again. And caring for Grady clearly opened up that possibility—it didn't matter where he spent his winters.

She couldn't do it. Wouldn't put herself through it. She'd rather die than hurt like that again.

Lex flopped over in her bed, nearly knocking Felicity off the end. The cat turned in a circle and settled again, farther away from Lex's feet. She wasn't purring like usual, but instead seemed to be staying close in order to give some feline moral support. Lex could use it.

No, what she could use was a good smack in the face for letting things get so out of hand with Grady. Within a matter of two months he'd gone from being an adversary to being a frenemy, from frenemy to friend and finally he'd become her lover.

But she hadn't expected the "love" part in "lover" to start taking hold.

It was, and she was in trouble if she didn't stop matters immediately. Before Grady started thinking he might be in love with her...if it wasn't already too late.

He was something of a romantic.

Well, she wasn't. She was realistic and practical. She knew what had to be done, and it was better done now than later. She assumed he was coming to talk tomorrow. He was as impatient by nature as she was.

The business would be finished, and she would go on with her life. It wouldn't take Grady long to bounce back. Unlike her, he made friends easily.

And she could hate that thought all she wanted, the fact remained that she couldn't allow herself to travel too far down the wrong road...the road that led to mind-numbing pain.

GRADY STOPPED BY Annie Get Your Gun the next morning after driving to Lex's place and finding her gone.

She was indeed at the store, getting ready to leave after dropping off some stuff she'd made.

"You want to talk," she said as he came into the store.

"You said we would." Danielle and Annie were in the back. He could hear their voices. One of them laughed lowly. What he wouldn't give to feel like laughing right now.

"The park?" It was on the other side of the back parking lot and seemed like an okay place, as long as it was relatively empty.

"That would do."

Lex led the way out the front door after calling out to Danielle that she was checking out for the day. It would have been shorter to go out the back, but apparently she wasn't up for being open about going somewhere with him—maybe to avoid questions later.

They walked along the alley next to the parking lot and crossed the street, then took seats side by side on the first park bench they came to. And there they sat in silence, a good foot of dark green metal between them, Grady with his forearms resting on his thighs, looking out across the park, Lex sitting stiffly beside him—each waiting for the other to start.

"So…" he finally said "…how are you?"

He turned in time to see her mouth quirk into a humorless smile. "I've been better."

"I'm sorry about the rodeo."

"It's more than that," she said, focusing on her hands, loosely clasped in her lap.

He had an idea of what *it* was after thinking over the events of the evening, remembering Lex's response to the announcer when he had helpfully mentioned to the crowd that Grady would be riding bulls soon. Not practice bulls, but the nasty kind. The best the stock contractors had to offer. "Are you worried? About me?"

She slowly turned her head toward him. "Of course I'm worried about you. I know you're good, but yeah, I'm worried."

"Do you want me to give up bull riding?" He'd lain awake for a long time wondering how he would feel about her answer to that question, but it was something he needed to know.

Her eyebrows drew together. "I wouldn't ask that of you."

Not the answer he'd expected. "Yet you're worried about me."

She nodded. Lex was not being Lex. She wasn't looking at him, wasn't challenging him. She was withdrawn in a way he'd never seen before. He reached out to touch her, and she looked at him, her expression troubled.

"What is it, Lex? What's the deal?"

Her frown deepened, and he had the feeling she wanted to say, *"I don't know,"* even though she did know. Or at least had an inkling. He wanted in on the secret, but she didn't say anything.

"I'll be back, you know. I'm going to winter here from now on. I may not get in the practice time, but…"

"It's not that, either," she said quickly.

"Then…?"

She raised her eyes to his, her expression deadly serious. "I don't need people the way other people need people." The words came blurting out.

"What?" Grady felt his stomach start to tighten. This wasn't a good development.

"Maybe I should have been clearer on this at the beginning." She looked away as she spoke, focusing on the back door of her store a hundred yards away.

"Maybe you should be clearer on it right now."

She drew in a breath and flexed her fingers as they lay on her thighs. "I don't do commitment, and because of that, I don't usually let things get too tight."

"Why not?"

The simple question seemed to throw her. "Because it's not the way I am. I told you. I don't need people the way other people need them."

"Bull." Her mouth tightened, and he watched as a stubborn expression formed. For better or for worse, the Lex he knew was coming back. "The only reason not to need people is that you're afraid of something." All he needed was to push her a little, and then they could deal with this matter in the usual way—by arguing.

"So?" She blinked at him as if he'd just made a pointless argument.

Now he was thrown, because he'd fully expected her to deny it and then he would explain to her why she was wrong. But no. She admitted it. Freely. "Well, maybe you need to deal with whatever it is you're afraid of."

"I am. I've found a way that works well for me and I'm sticking with it."

"And that way is?"

"Not getting involved in committed relationships. It's not fair to the other person…who in this case would be you."

"That's crazy."

"That's logical. I don't want to get hurt, so I don't get too involved."

"What if you do get…involved?"

"I do what I'm doing right now."

"Just turn off your feelings?"

"Before they get to the point that I can't. Yes."

He blinked at her, not certain if he was sad or frustrated. He definitely felt a degree of both. How did a guy fight this? "Turning off feelings won't work in the long run."

"It's working just fine now, and that's all I care about."

"Lex—"

"I made no promises," she said fiercely. "I loved our time together, but I know what I have to do to survive." She got to her feet.

"Walk away? Shut down?"

"It works."

"This is it?" he asked incredulously.

"I can't see what else it can be."

"But…"

"I'm sorry, Grady. I shouldn't have let things go this far." She ducked her chin briefly, then raised it again. "I need to go." She marched out of the park toward her truck parked on the street behind Annie Get Your Gun without so much as a backward glance.

Grady leaned back against the bench, letting his hands drop loosely on either side of him.

LEX WAS GLAD she made it to her truck without throwing up or something. She was that stressed, which only went to prove that, no, she should not be in a relationship. She didn't do well starting them or ending them.

The middle part wasn't bad.

Middles didn't last forever. Lex jammed the truck into gear. She told herself she wasn't going to look, but she did. Grady was still sitting on the bench. She'd hated hurting him, but this was only a small hurt. Not a hole-in-your-heart hurt. Not a hope-you-said-a-proper-good-bye-because-you'll-never-see-him-again hurt.

Even if Grady quit bull riding, the possibility was there of reopening that agonizing chasm. Things happened and, when dealing with a risk taker like Grady... yes. Things happened.

And this time maybe she wouldn't heal so well. How many times could a person bounce back from a broken heart?

Lex didn't intend to be a guinea pig for that study.

When she got home, she walked into the house, with the dogs and Felicity swirling around her feet. They were careful not to trip her but got as close as possible. Perfect analogy for her and Grady. She'd tried to get as close as possible without tripping up. She'd tripped anyhow, and now they both had to deal with it.

Did he love her?

He might think he did. But by the time she was done establishing distance between them, he probably wouldn't think so any longer. He'd gotten over Danielle. He'd get over her, too.

If he thought he loved her. She didn't even know if he did.

All she knew was that it was very possible she was in love with him, and she needed to get over that.

Step one had been taken.

Chapter Fourteen

Grady figured if he gave Lex some time, she'd realize that she was reacting to stress, but after not hearing from her for two days, he took a chance and called her. Bad move.

She was distantly polite and the conversation ended after a few stiff exchanges, which frustrated the heck out of him. How was he supposed to deal with polite Lex? He'd never before encountered polite Lex. If she'd treated him that way from day one, they probably never would have hooked up and that would have saved him some heartache.

Annie obviously knew something was up, possibly from the way Grady was now attacking his daily workouts, doubling his reps, his running time, and also coming home at a decent hour, never spending the night anywhere except her guest room. She kept giving him the look—the sister look—which he in turn pretended not to notice. The one thing he didn't want to do was to discuss the situation with Lex.

"Are you still coming back?" Annie asked after he'd helped her load the dishwasher.

"Of course. I've been pricing trailers. Why?"

Annie pulled a pan out of the drain rack and dried

it. "I just wondered, now that you and Lex aren't... seeing so much of each other, if you might not find Oklahoma more to your liking."

She kept wiping the pan until Grady took it out of her hands and set it on the counter. "Being here is to my liking. I want to settle here. Watch the girls grow up. Whether I stay or go has nothing to do with Lex."

"She's back to the way she was when I found her scary," Annie commented as she once again picked up the pan and this time stowed it in a cupboard near the stove.

"Sorry about that. I did my best to keep that from happening."

"It was bad?" Annie asked, still holding the dish towel as she dropped her hands to her sides.

"Yeah. Bad."

"I'm sorry."

He tilted up one corner of his mouth in an attempt at a smile, but it drifted back down again. "And I'm sorry I keep screwing up things with the women you work with."

Annie gave a small shrug. "They don't seem to hold it against me."

"Small mercies, eh?"

HENNESSEY'S BECAME GRADY'S SANCTUARY. He showed up early, stayed late, practicing and helping the young riders. Not one person said a word about Lex. Unless he initiated the conversation, not that many people engaged him period. Catching an unexpected glimpse of himself in a truck mirror, he understood why. He looked as if he was about to do someone bodily harm. His riding, however, seemed to benefit from the frustration he carried with him every waking moment of the day. He approached each ride with an aggression he hadn't felt prior to Lex giving him his walking orders.

Then came the day she showed up at Hennessey's just as he was leaving one late afternoon. His heart thumped hard at the sight of her standing near his truck, but when he got close enough to see her closed-off expression, he knew this wasn't going to be a joyful I've-rethought-things reunion. She held out a bag.

"Some stuff you left at my place."

The symbolic returning of all things left behind.

Grady took the bag, somehow keeping himself from snatching it out of her hands. It was now or never. Lex was not going to soften toward him over time. If anything, she was going to convince herself that she'd done the only thing possible—because she was afraid of doing anything else.

"We can work this out."

"I'm good with the way things are," she replied, adjusting her sunglasses.

"You're good not needing people? Or not needing me?"

She let out a soft sigh that smacked of frustration and then sidestepped his question. "I can't change who I am."

He smirked at her; he couldn't help himself. This was the Lex who had threatened to take him down if he hurt Danielle. The Lex that hid behind a cool facade and couldn't be reasoned with. He had to try. "Why are you so certain that I'll hurt you?"

Her cool slipped a little then. "Circumstances will hurt me, Grady. Things we can't control."

"Like me getting taken out by a bull?"

"Yes, that. But there's more behind my decision."

"Fill me in," he muttered from between his teeth as a couple of young riders walked by.

"I'm happy with my life the way it is. I'm sorry you can't accept that I don't want to hook up with anyone for any length of time, but that's the way it is. I know you think that if you chip away you can make me realize that you're worth the risk, but…" She shook her head slowly.

"You're a coward, Lex."

"I'm honest to myself, Grady."

"Dream on." He brushed past her to get into his truck, and she turned at the same time to march to her rig.

And so it ends.

He jammed the key into the ignition, and his truck roared to life. And then he dropped his chin and forced himself to take a breath. Focus on what he was doing, not on what he was losing.

THE NEXT DAY when Annie got home from work, he presented her with the rototiller he'd bought her, which was sitting in the middle of the twenty-foot-square area he'd turned over next to her much smaller garden. He'd thought about putting a ribbon on top, but instead he found several of the silk flowers he'd used on Katie's pink hair, wrapped the stems in duct tape and taped them to the handle. Annie burst out laughing when she saw the bouquet.

"You do have a way with flowers."

"I hope you don't mind that I broke the thing in for you," he said.

She gave him a big hug. "Not. One. Bit." Then she toed up to the edge of the freshly tilled earth and put her hands to her cheeks. "I'm going to have such a garden next year."

"I figured that this gives you room to grow melons and pumpkins if you want."

"It does."

"And honestly? I should be here to help plant next spring."

"We should be able to get the garden in before you start your spring circuit," she agreed. Then she let out a sigh. "Remember—I totally get it if you need to winter elsewhere. I can't handle being a project or a duty."

"Noted." He gave her one last squeeze before stepping back.

Annie brushed the hair out of her eyes. "The girls are giving you a surprise going-away party tomorrow. They planned it themselves."

"That's cool."

"They wanted to invite Lex, but I made up an excuse. Just so you know."

"Thank you."

The twins' party was cute. They'd been very busy in the kitchen an hour or so before Annie got home, but nothing broke or spilled. After Annie got home and changed her clothes, they'd made a big deal about sitting Grady at the table, complete with tablecloth and flowers with no duct tape. They carefully poured Kool-Aid into the good china cups, then offered Grady his choice of Oreo cookies, Chips Ahoy or vanilla wafers to go with his ice cream and chocolate syrup.

"Dinner's a no-go tonight?" he asked Annie as she

handed Kristen a dish of ice cream to deliver to the table. Katie was waiting for the next.

"Sometimes you gotta say 'what the hey' and have ice cream for dinner," she said as she dug into the carton for another scoop.

"My kind of woman."

"It's a special 'casion," Kristen explained. "Sometimes you don't have to eat supper on special 'casions."

"Well, thank you for this special party," Grady said as Kristen dropped two Oreos on top of his ice cream.

"We know you're coming back, but it'll be a long time from now," Katie said.

"Three months."

"Almost until Christmas!" Kristen rolled her eyes, telling Grady how far away that was in the kid brain. He happened to know that Annie was counting the paychecks until Christmas arrived and thought it was coming way too soon.

"We're going to miss you." The girls spoke in unison without seeming to notice, then took their chairs on either side of Grady. They were looking glum for being in the midst of a special 'casion.

"How about I'll send you postcards from the cities I visit?"

"Postcards?" Two pairs of interested gazes met his.

"In the mail." What a novelty to the digital generation. "I buy a postcard with a picture of where I'm at, write a message, put a stamp on it and mail it to you guys."

Katie grinned. "Can we each get a postcard?"

"I don't know…they're almost twenty-five cents each…" He pretended to debate, then nodded. "One each. From each city." They clapped their hands and he smiled. He was going to miss this. "I know—let's print out a map and your mom can show you where each card comes from."

The twins were all over that, and he didn't have to print out a map because Annie found an old road map of the USA in her junk drawer. Grady and the girls mounted it on their bedroom wall and he made a red dot on Gavin, Montana, and another on New York City.

The girls had no concept of the distance involved, but they agreed that it looked like a long way away.

"Will you send Lex postcards, too?" Kristen asked matter-of-factly.

Grady met Annie's gaze over the top of the twins' head. "I, uh…might."

"She'll like that," Katie said.

Somehow he didn't think so.

The next morning he was loading his duffels into his truck, when Danielle's car pulled into Annie's drive. It was barely seven, so Grady was justifiably surprised to see her.

"Everything all right?" he asked as she got out of the car. Because the only reason he could think of for her to be there was to see him, since she'd see Annie at work within the hour.

"You're heading out now?" she asked instead of answering his question.

"I catch a flight to New York later this afternoon." The Hayward twins were going to pick up his rig at the airport and bring it back to Annie's.

"I'd hoped to talk to you before you left."

He opened his hands in a here-I-am gesture.

"It's about Lex." She hesitated, perhaps giving him time to say that he didn't want to talk about Lex. He didn't want to talk about her, but since Danielle had come all this way, he'd listen.

"Yeah?"

"She's scared of loss."

"Aren't we all?"

"You know this stems from what happened with her dad."

"I figured." He put a hand on the bed of his truck and considered the ground at his feet. He looked up to see Danielle frowning at him, as if hoping he'd say something like *"Don't worry, I know how to handle this."* He didn't. "I did everything I could to make being with me an okay thing. I even offered to give up bull riding."

"Really?" It was hard to miss the note of quiet incredulity.

"Yeah. Sorry."

"No," she replied hurriedly. "It's okay. It worked out for the best. I'm simply…surprised."

"I care for her."

"She cares for you."

"Not enough." He could see that she was going to rush to the defense of her friend, so he put up a hand. "I know she's scared. I know there are issues, but there's not much I can do about it when she shuts me out. As I see it, the problem is that she doesn't care for me enough to confront the issues keeping us apart."

It hadn't been easy to accept that truth—in fact, it had taken him over a week to finally come to grips with the obvious, but once he had, his course of action had become clear. He needed to get on with his life.

"She needs time."

He shook his head. "Time isn't going to help. She's

decided that if she doesn't feel, then she won't get hurt."

"Like that's going to work."

"She thinks it will."

Danielle gave him a sympathetic look. "Sorry she feels that way."

So was he, but he was done beating his head on a wall.

"Well, at least one of us is happy," Grady said, working up a smile for the woman he'd once thought to be the most perfect on earth, before he'd met the imperfect woman who'd stolen his heart. Stomped on it. Walked away.

Danielle smiled back. He opened his arms, and she walked into his embrace, hugging him hard. "Congratulations," he murmured. "Curtis is a lucky guy."

She pulled back, holding him by the shoulders. "Thank you. And good luck to you."

He didn't know if she meant with the bulls or getting over Lex. Either way, he needed it.

IT DIDN'T TAKE a rocket scientist to deduce that Danielle and Annie were either angry at her or felt sorry for her. Maybe both.

Lex laid out the jewelry she'd finished making the night before in a marathon session in her basement. They were good pieces—pieces that Tiffani would probably enjoy because Lex had incorporated shiny things in the design.

Grady was gone, headed off to NYC, the first stop of the Bull Extravaganza, with the intent of returning to Gavin in early winter. Danielle had filled her in as if they were discussing a mutual acquaintance instead of her former lover—the guy she'd intended to have fun with before he moved on. The guy she now couldn't get out of her head.

But she would.

All she had to do was to focus on other matters, as she'd done after her dad died. It had taken some time, but eventually she'd edged back to normality. Or a state that closely resembled normality. Did it once, she could do it again.

And in the future, she was going to avoid falling in love.

"These are nice." Annie stopped next to her to admire as she hung a pair of copper earrings shaped like boots with hearts cut out of the center and small crystals hanging in the hearts.

"New design," Lex said, glad that Grady's sister was making the attempt to talk to her. "I'm trying to branch out."

"Seek new horizons?" Annie asked. Lex shot her a glance, wondering if there was another meaning behind the words, but Annie's expression was clear.

"Keeping myself busy," she said honestly. She was all about keeping busy. Enjoying the life she'd made for herself—the store, her farm. Her animals.

Annie held up a bracelet loaded with whimsical Western charms. "I might have you make something special for the twins' birthday if you take special orders."

"I'd be happy to."

"I have a few months, but I think something Western like this, but smaller, of course."

"I'll bring in my charm catalogue," Lex said, glad

that things with Annie seemed to be moving back toward the way they were before she and Grady had hooked up—and that was how she had to think of it. As a hookup.

Later that afternoon during a lull, Lex and Danielle worked on the wedding favors while Annie ran to the school to help with a library hour. And even though it was only the two of them, the back room of the store didn't feel as comfortable as usual. Danielle was deep in thought, her movements quick, almost jerky. Lex was about to ask her if everything was okay between her and Curtis when Danielle suddenly leveled a look at her. A suck-in-a-breath-and-go-for-it look. "You know I'm your friend."

Lex pressed her lips together and concentrated on tying a bow. Any conversation that started like that was bound to be uncomfortable. As in one that might address things she'd yet to fully come to terms with. "I know," she said.

"As your friend, I feel that I can say that I'm concerned about you. About this thing with Grady."

Lex set down the tulle bag. "Because we broke up?"

"Because of the reason why you broke up."

Lex narrowed her eyes. "We broke up because I didn't want to see him anymore." Which was entirely her call, her business.

"Because...?"

Lex rolled her eyes. "In the long run it wasn't going to work."

Danielle cinched a circle of tulle shut, knotted it and reached for another. "With Grady? Or with anyone?"

"What does that mean?"

"It means that I'm concerned about you shutting down emotionally in order to avoid pain."

Lex reached for a roll of ribbon and unrolled about four times more than she needed. "What if I feel better when I'm shut down?"

"Better for how long?"

Lex started chopping the ribbon into more manageable lengths. "I don't know…the rest of my life?" Now the ribbon was too short. She brushed the pieces into the garbage can with a sweep of her hand.

"You need to think about what you're doing."

"I know what I'm doing." Although she was a bit concerned by what Danielle was doing. Never, in their long years of friendship, had Danielle gotten tough with her.

"I always thought of you as an honest person, Lex. Too honest most of the time."

"Guilty." And why weren't any customers coming into the store to rescue her from this conversation?

"So I want you to be honest with yourself now." Danielle put down the tulle and leaned onto her forearms, her expression serious. "Are you lying to yourself?"

"About?"

Danielle held her gaze. "Anything." The single word hung between them.

Lex pulled in a breath, set her scissors down and stood. For a moment she faced off with her friend across the work table, telling herself that Danielle didn't understand. She hadn't lost a loved one. She didn't understand the depth of pain involved…

But Danielle hadn't been talking about loss. She'd been talking about honesty.

And Lex didn't have an answer. Not an honest one, anyway.

The customers started coming then, trickling in one after another. Tourists and locals. Danielle's grandmother stopped by to show her a photo of a veil, and Lex couldn't bring herself to join them as she normally would have done. She needed some time. Some space.

After Annie got back close to closing time, she took off as she'd originally intended to do.

She stopped at the feed store to buy dog food, cat food, alfalfa pellets and rolled oats and almost asked for a bag of Nancy's special duck food. She missed having the ducks and had thought more than once about getting a few of her own in the spring—except that the ducks reminded her of Grady and the first time they made love.

It'd been a mistake. A miscalculation on her part.

She'd thought going in that they'd make love a time or two and when the novelty wore off, they'd part as friends. Or friendly nemeses, or something along those lines.

The novelty hadn't worn off. It had changed into something deeper, something she hadn't been prepared for. Something she was afraid of losing and was therefore afraid of embracing.

You're a coward, Lex.

Grady's words sounded in her head at least a dozen times a day, first thoroughly irritating her then making her think. Did protecting herself give her coward status?

She refused to believe that. But refusing to believe it didn't give her any sense of peace.

Nothing gave her a sense of peace.

The twins came by the shop after school, looking adorable in polka-dot dresses, Kristen's red with white and Katie's white with red.

"We don't usually wear matching dresses," Katie explained to Lex when she complimented them.

"'Cept special 'casions. We're going to Julie's birthday party."

Lex agreed that special occasions called for special dresses, and then Kristen said, "Do you miss Uncle Grady?"

Only when she was awake. Okay—that wasn't quite true, since she also dreamed about him.

"I do," she admitted.

"He's riding the bulls now. We saw him on TV!"

"He's really brave," Katie added.

He was brave. He rode bulls, and he wasn't afraid of emotions. He embraced everything, while Lex hid from the most challenging and rewarding arena in life. The feeling part.

And doing that kept her sane. Everyone had their survival strategies. Despite what Danielle thought, she was being honest with herself. Not everyone would agree with her strategies, but they worked for her.

The weeks marched on, first one, then two, then three. She finally gave in to temptation, looked up Grady's rides in the Bull Extravaganza, telling herself it was a step in her healing process. A small part of her actually tried to believe it. He hadn't won any legs of the competition yet, but he'd earned some respectable scores. The banner on the Bull Extravaganza site helpfully listed the next stop on the tour and the time it would be televised.

Lex closed out of the site and leaned back in her chair. Did she want to watch?

Her instant stomachache told her no.

Was she tough enough to watch?

Two days later she found out when she tuned into the show, just in time to see Grady accepting a buckle for that leg of the tour and then getting a major lip-lock from a gorgeous redhead. His hand slid down around the redhead's waist to the top of her hip and even though it was a perfectly normal thing to do during a kiss, Lex was instantly conscious of an emotion that rarely cropped up in her life.

Jealousy.

She couldn't tear her eyes away from Grady, the familiar smile, his eyes crinkling at the corners as he spoke to the interviewer. Yes, he'd taken a break from PBR, so he was happy to have this opportunity to join the Bull Extravaganza. No, the break hadn't hurt his form or his concentration and no, he didn't see retirement anywhere in the near future.

Grady accepted the interviewer's good luck wishes and kissed the redhead one more time, and Lex turned off the television.

Sleep did not come easily tonight. Or the following night.

When her dad died, it had been done. Over. No fixing the situation. But Grady was still there—living life, taking chances, haunting her dreams…kissing redheads.

Time. This would pass with time.

Except she'd given it time, and if anything she felt worse than when she'd ended their relationship to keep from being hurt. She'd given up the possibility of happiness to avoid the possibility of pain.

Grady was right.

She was a coward.

Chapter Fifteen

It hadn't been easy to get herself into the gates of the Bull Extravaganza—and it would have been impossible if she hadn't been Luke Benjamin's daughter. The bullfighters at the extravaganza were the best in the business and several of them knew her father. A few phone calls and she was able to not only get in the doors, but to get a ride to the arena, sharing a taxi with one of her dad's oldest professional friends, Wild Bill Johnson.

"First rodeo?" Bill asked.

Lex knew exactly what he meant. First since her father had died. "No...but I didn't make it through the bull riding."

"You won't have a lot of choice today, if you insist on going through those gates."

"I know. I need to go."

"Clear things out of your system?"

"Yes." She hadn't told him about Grady—only that she had a friend riding and it was important that she be there.

Bill reached over and patted her shoulder. "It'll be all right, kid. The first rodeo is the hardest."

It was hard. The first few rides had Lex's heart

in her throat and her stomach in a tight knot, but she hadn't thrown up as she'd feared. The bullfighters on this competition were extraordinary, knowing exactly how to distract the bull away from the downed bull rider in the most efficient manner. Her father had been a master at that. He'd also been at the end of his game. At forty-five, he should have been retired, but he'd been one of those athletes who had defied time.

Until it caught up with him.

As Grady's ride approached, the calmness she'd faked herself into evaporated. She forced herself to breathe. Grady did this for a living. He was good at it. Really good. She'd be stupid not to be concerned, but she had faith in his abilities, even if he'd drawn a rank bull. She wasn't familiar with No M.O., but a bullfighter's son filled her in. "Dad hates that bull," the kid said at the end of his dissertation. Lex stretched her mouth into a smile of acknowledgment and focused on her breathing. She could do this.

She had to do this.

GRADY WAS BEGINNING to wonder if a little of his sister's recent hard luck hadn't rubbed off on him. He'd done okay during the first few stops of the Bull Extravaganza, had won a leg, but the current stop wasn't starting out so well. His luggage had gotten lost, so all he had to his name was the grip bag with his rope, glove, rosin, vest and spurs. His chaps had been in the checked bag—a mistake he'd never make again—so he'd had to borrow. Green batwings with metallic pink fringe. Lots of it. Flashy, to say the least, and almost too long, so he had to watch how he walked. And then he'd drawn No M.O., perhaps the rankest bull on the circuit. If Grady could do his part he'd be in the money, because the bull always scored high, but that was the trick. No M.O. was so named because he didn't have one—an M.O., or modus operandi, that is. He changed up his routine, sometimes rearing out of the chute, sometimes charging a few feet, then throwing himself into spins, first one way, then the other, and sometimes he simply short hopped before launching into some nasty twisting bucks.

Grady spent the last minutes of his warm-up time stretching, going over the ride in his mind. Tamping down the fear, because in his book, only fools weren't afraid. He never watched the other riders until after his ride, didn't want their victories or errors getting into his head.

The house was packed, as it generally was for the specialty bull-riding events, but the crowd seemed unreal during his prep. There, but not. He enjoyed the cheers, the positive vibes, but he was never really conscious of being watched until he rode for eight and then allowed himself to look outside the bubble of concentration he'd created. If he landed on his butt, the only people in his world were the bullfighters, the other riders, the gate men. The judges. There was no embarrassment, no shame.

Grady paced behind the chute until No M.O. was loaded. Then he adjusted his belled rope and eased on, pounding his gloved left fist tight around the rope with his right hand. That was when the calm came, blocking out everything except for the feel of the warm flesh and powerful muscles shifting and twitching beneath him, ready to explode when the gate opened and the flank strap tightened.

Grady nodded, and No M.O. reared out of the gate almost before it was open, planted his front feet and attempted to swing his backside over his ears. After that a series of quick spins to the right, followed by a change of direction and quick spins to the left, drool flying off his muzzle.

He had this one. Instinct told him when the whistle would blow. A fraction of a second later it sounded, and he was still in the center of the bull.

Lex gripped the edge of her seat hard. Even though Grady was still on top, she couldn't relax, because this was the part of the bull ride she was conditioned to fear—the part after the whistle. The part where her dad could have gotten hurt.

Grady was checking out his dismount, and Lex was beginning to think she could allow herself to breathe again when the bull did a sudden twisting kick and flipped Grady over his hand onto the wrong side of the animal. His feet beat on the ground as the bull started spinning, tossing Grady against his side like a rag doll as he fought desperately to get his feet under him so he could free his trapped wrist.

Lex jumped up, hand pressed hard over her chest.

Wild Bill dashed at the animal, taunting him, luring him out of the spins and into a straight line, allowing Grady to finally get his feet under himself. Grady made a grab for the tail of the rope as the bull charged Wild Bill, caught it as his feet went out from under him again. He managed a yank and broke free, falling to his knees in the dirt as the second bullfighter dodged a hook and kept the bull from coming around and charging Grady.

Thus thwarted, the bull tossed his head, kinked his tail and trotted toward the exit gate, his work done for the next several weeks. For a long moment, Grady stayed where he was, on his knees in the middle of the arena. He shook his head, then slowly got to his feet and headed toward the fence. The crowd cheered wildly, for Grady, for the bullfighters, for the bull.

Lex was apparently the only one in the audience with tears streaming down her face.

"GOOD TO GO."

Grady had known that before the medic checked him out, even though his shoulder had come close to being dislocated and his wrist was turning blue as it swelled up. Might be a sprain, might be a fracture. They'd have to wait for the swelling to diminish to know for sure.

With the green and pink chaps slung over his shoulder, he collected his gear, automatically checked his phone before shoving it in his pocket, then almost dropped it when he saw the text from Lex.

I need to see you. Tonight if you aren't hurting too bad.

Tonight?
Where are you? he texted back, heart thumping against his ribs as he waited for the reply.

Here. With Sam Mitchell's son. Near west exit.

Grady didn't bother to reply. He worked his way through a small crowd of riders outside the changing room, rounded the end of the holding area, grimacing as a guy with a camera bumped his shoulder, then headed toward the west exit.

"Grady!"

He stopped, turned. And there she was, looking like something out of one of his dreams, dressed in jeans and boots and a lace top, her dark hair falling over one shoulder. Looking so good that he hoped against hell he wasn't having some kind of hallucination; that his brain hadn't been beat to the point that he was imagining things.

Her chin moved as she swallowed; then she started toward him, her expression a mixture of determination and uncertainty. But what struck him most was that her eyes were red. She'd been crying.

Lex. Crying.

That did him in. Grady closed the last couple of feet between them, wrapping his good arm around her, burying his face in her hair as he held her tightly, thinking how crazy this was. Lex was here. She pressed more tightly against him, and he felt her shudder.

"It's okay," he murmured. "It's okay." What on earth had she been putting herself through that she'd been crying? How many demons had she confronted by coming here?

She nodded against his shoulder, and damned if he didn't feel dampness there.

When she finally pulled back, there were indeed tears glistening on her dark lashes. She blinked those gorgeous eyes at him but didn't say a word. There was no need. He got it.

"Would it be too soon to tell you that I love you?" he asked.

She shook her head, and he figured she was afraid that if she answered, she'd start crying for real. In public. Not a Lex thing.

"I have to stay until the show's over," he said, running his hand up and down her arm, then brushing her hair back over her shoulder before cupping his palm against her face and leaning down to kiss her. A soft kiss. An it's-all-right kiss that deepened into an I-can't-imagine-life-without-you kiss.

"I've got things I have to tell you," she said when he lifted his head. "Important things."

His stomach tightened, but he nodded. "We can talk later. In private."

"This can't wait…I was wrong."

"About what?"

"Needing. I wasn't being honest with myself. People need other people. And I need you."

"Of course you do," he said in an attempt at cockiness. The effect was ruined by the fact that he felt like crying himself. "But no more than I need you."

A smile trembled on Lex's lips. "I was hoping you wouldn't tell me to take a hike."

"Not a chance. This has all been really hard for me, but—" he gave a small shrug "—what doesn't kill you makes you stronger, and I've kind of been feeling like Superman lately."

"Sorry about that." She reached out to take his good hand, running her thumb over the back of it. "Can I stay with you until the show is over?"

"I wouldn't have it any other way."

And so it was. Grady kept Lex's hand in his as they waited for the announcement of the winner—not him, but he'd been close—and the presentation of the buckle. Then, after the longest bull event of his career, he had Lex all to himself on the taxi ride back to his hotel, and she hadn't let go of his hand once. She was, however, a little more herself once they hit his room, where his luggage was waiting.

"You can imagine my relief when I discovered those pink and green chaps weren't yours," she said.

"They were kind of pretty under the lights."

"And had nice movement as you were flopping along the bull's side."

"Funny."

She took his face in her hands, both frowning and smiling as she said, "I'm afraid to touch you anywhere else."

"Take a chance. I'll tell you if it hurts."

"You know what?" she said with a lift of her eyebrows.

"What?"

"I'm going to do the same."

She wasn't talking bruises—not the physical kind, anyway—and hearing those words made his heart almost explode. "You know I'm here for you."

"And that is the most amazing thing, Grady. I figured that you'd probably written me off."

"I tried. It didn't work."

"Same here." She leaned her forehead against his. "Guess that means we're stuck with each other?"

He smiled against her lips. "Can't think of anyone I'd rather be stuck with. I love you, Lex."

"Not one bit more than I love you."

* * * * *

#1589 TEXAS REBELS: JUDE

Texas Rebels • by Linda Warren

When Paige Wheeler returns to the small Texas town where she grew up, will Jude Rebel be able to tell her he kept the child she gave up for adoption...or will he continue to protect his heart?

#1590 FALLING FOR THE RANCHER

Cupid's Bow, Texas • by Tanya Michaels

Rancher Jarrett Ross is a man who blames himself for putting his sister in a wheelchair. Hiring physical therapist Sierra Bailey means Sierra's off-limits—no matter how much he wants her.

#1591 A COWBOY'S CLAIM

Cowboys of the Rio Grande • by Marin Thomas

When rodeo cowboy Victor Vicario is given temporary custody of his nephew, he asks barrel racer Tanya McGee for help. Victor knows it can't last, but their little family *feels* real...

#1592 THE ACCIDENTAL COWBOY

Angel Crossing, Arizona • by Heidi Hormel

When former bronc rider Lavonda Leigh agrees to guide an archaeologist through rough ranch terrain, she's not expecting a smoldering Scottish cowboy! Jones Kincaid is sure to dig up trouble in Arizona...

REQUEST YOUR FREE BOOKS!
2 FREE NOVELS PLUS 2 FREE GIFTS!

❤ HARLEQUIN®

American Romance®

LOVE, HOME & HAPPINESS

YES! Please send me 2 FREE Harlequin® American Romance® novels and my 2 FREE gifts (gifts are worth about $10). After receiving them, if I don't wish to receive any more books, I can return the shipping statement marked "cancel." If I don't cancel, I will receive 4 brand-new novels every month and be billed just $4.74 per book in the U.S. or $5.49 per book in Canada. That's a savings of at least 12% off the cover price! It's quite a bargain! Shipping and handling is just 50¢ per book in the U.S. and 75¢ per book in Canada.* I understand that accepting the 2 free books and gifts places me under no obligation to buy anything. I can always return a shipment and cancel at any time. Even if I never buy another book, the two free books and gifts are mine to keep forever.

154/354 HDN GHZZ

Name	(PLEASE PRINT)

Address	Apt. #

City	State/Prov.	Zip/Postal Code

Signature (if under 18, a parent or guardian must sign)

Mail to the **Reader Service:**
IN U.S.A.: P.O. Box 1867, Buffalo, NY 14240-1867
IN CANADA: P.O. Box 609, Fort Erie, Ontario L2A 5X3

Want to try two free books from another line?
Call 1-800-873-8635 or visit www.ReaderService.com.

* Terms and prices subject to change without notice. Prices do not include applicable taxes. Sales tax applicable in N.Y. Canadian residents will be charged applicable taxes. Offer not valid in Quebec. This offer is limited to one order per household. Not valid for current subscribers to Harlequin American Romance books. All orders subject to credit approval. Credit or debit balances in a customer's account(s) may be offset by any other outstanding balance owed by or to the customer. Please allow 4 to 6 weeks for delivery. Offer available while quantities last.

Your Privacy—The Reader Service is committed to protecting your privacy. Our Privacy Policy is available online at www.ReaderService.com or upon request from the Reader Service.

We make a portion of our mailing list available to reputable third parties that offer products we believe may interest you. If you prefer that we not exchange your name with third parties, or if you wish to clarify or modify your communication preferences, please visit us at www.ReaderService.com/consumerchoice or write to us at Reader Service Preference Service, P.O. Box 9062, Buffalo, NY 14240-9062. Include your complete name and address.

Jude parked at the curb of the new Horseshoe Park and
made his way to where he saw Paige sitting at a picnic
table. The first thing he'd noticed was she was slimmer
and her hair was more blond than brown. It suited her.
Her face still held that same sweet innocence that had
first attracted him to her. But now there was a maturity
about her that was just as attractive.

She got up and ran to him, then wrapped her arms
around his waist and hugged him. He froze, which was
more the reaction of the boy he used to be. But the man in
him recognized all those old feelings that had bound him
to her years ago. Maybe some things just never changed.

When he didn't return the hug, she went back to
the table and he eased onto the bench across from her,
removing his hat. The wind rustled through the tall oaks
and he took a moment to gather his thoughts. It was like

gathering bits and pieces from his past to guide him. What should he say? What should he do?

"You look good," she said. "You filled out. The teenage boy I used to date doesn't seem to exist anymore."

"He grew up, and so have you. The young girl of long ago has matured into a beautiful woman."

"Thank you." She tilted her head slightly to smile at him and his heart raced like a wild mustang's at the look he remembered well. "You were always good for my ego."

He didn't shift or act nervous. He had to be the man he was supposed to be. For Zane. And for himself.

"How's California?"

"Great. I'm busy, so I don't get to see a lot of it. But I've enjoyed my stay there."

"I'm glad you had the chance to make your dream come true." He meant that with all his heart. But a small part of him wanted her to love him enough to have stayed and raised their son together. "Do you still work on the ranch?" she asked quickly, as if she wanted to change the subject.

"Yes. I'll always be a cowboy."

She fiddled with her hands in her lap. "I heard you have a son." Her eyes caught his, and all the guilt hit him, blindsiding him.

"Yes." *Our son. The one you gave away.*

Don't miss TEXAS REBELS: JUDE
by Linda Warren,
available April 2016 everywhere
Harlequin® American Romance®
books and ebooks are sold.

www.Harlequin.com

JUST CAN'T GET ENOUGH?

Join our social communities
and talk to us online.

You will have access to the latest
news on upcoming titles and special
promotions, but most importantly,
you can talk to other fans about your
favorite Harlequin reads.

Harlequin.com/Community

Facebook.com/HarlequinBooks

Twitter.com/HarlequinBooks

Pinterest.com/HarlequinBooks

THE WORLD IS BETTER WITH

Romance

Harlequin has everything from contemporary, passionate and heartwarming to suspenseful and inspirational stories.

Whatever your mood, we have a romance just for you!

Connect with us to find your next great read, special offers and more.

f /HarlequinBooks

🐦 @HarlequinBooks

www.HarlequinBlog.com

www.Harlequin.com/Newsletters

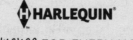

◆ HARLEQUIN®

A *Romance* FOR EVERY MOOD™

www.Harlequin.com